Eli Manning

Other books in the People in the News series:

Maya Angelou

Tyra Banks

David Beckham

Beyoncé

Fidel Castro

Kelly Clarkson

Hillary Clinton

Miley Cyrus

Ellen Degeneres

Hilary Duff

Zac Efron

Brett Favre

50 Cent

Al Gore

Tony Hawk

Salma Hayek

LeBron James

Jay-Z

Derek Jeter

Steve Jobs

Dwayne Johnson

Angelina Jolie

Jonas Brothers

Kim Jong II

Coretta Scott King

Ashton Kutcher

Tobey Maguire

Eli Manning

John McCain

Barack Obama

Michelle Obama

Danica Patrick

Nancy Pelosi

Queen Latifah

Daniel Radcliffe

Condoleezza Rice

Rihanna

J K. Rowling

Shakira

Tupac Shakur

Will Smith

Gwen Stefani

Ben Stiller

Hilary Swank

Justin Timberlake

Usher

Denzel Washington

Oprah Winfrey

Eli
Manning

by John F. Wukovits

LUCENT BOOKS
A part of Gale, Cengage Learning

GALE
CENGAGE Learning

Detroit • New York • San Francisco • New Haven, Conn • Waterville, Maine • London

LIBRARY OF CONGRESS CATALOGING-IN-PUBLICATION DATA

Wukovits, John F., 1944–
  Eli Manning / by John F. Wukovits.
    p. cm. — (People in the news)
  Includes bibliographical references and index.
  ISBN 978-1-4205-0241-1 (hardcover)
1. Manning, Eli, 1981—Juvenile literature. 2. Football players—United States—Biography—Juvenile literature. 3. Quarterbacks (Football)—United States—Biography—Juvenile literature. I. Title.
  GV939.M2887W85 2010
  796.332092—dc22
  [B]

2009036536

Lucent Books
27500 Drake Rd
Farmington Hills MI 48331

ISBN-13: 978-1-4205-0241-1
ISBN-10: 1-4205-0241-7

Printed in the United States of America
1 2 3 4 5 6 7 14 13 12 11 10

Printed by Bang Printing, Brainerd, MN, 1ˢᵗ Ptg., 03/2010

Contents

Fame and celebrity are alluring. People are drawn to those who walk in fame's spotlight, whether they are known for great accomplishments or for notorious deeds. The lives of the famous pique public interest and attract attention, perhaps because their experiences seem in some ways so different from, yet in other ways so similar to, our own.

Newspapers, magazines, and television regularly capitalize on this fascination with celebrity by running profiles of famous people. For example, television programs such as *Entertainment Tonight* devote all their programming to stories about entertainment and entertainers. Magazines such as *People* fill their pages with stories of the private lives of famous people. Even newspapers, newsmagazines, and television news frequently delve into the lives of well-known personalities. Despite the number of articles and programs, few provide more than a superficial glimpse at their subjects.

Lucent's People in the News series offers young readers a deeper look into the lives of today's newsmakers, the influences that have shaped them, and the impact they have had in their fields of endeavor and on other people's lives. The subjects of the series hail from many disciplines and walks of life. They include authors, musicians, athletes, political leaders, entertainers, entrepreneurs, and others who have made a mark on modern life and who, in many cases, will continue to do so for years to come.

These biographies are more than factual chronicles. Each book emphasizes the contributions, accomplishments, or deeds that have brought fame or notoriety to the individual and shows how that person has influenced modern life. Authors portray their subjects in a realistic, unsentimental light. For example, Bill Gates—the cofounder of the software giant Microsoft—has been instrumental in making personal computers the most vital tool of the modern age. Few dispute his business savvy, his perseverance, or his technical expertise, yet critics say he is ruthless in his dealings with competitors and driven more by his desire to maintain Microsoft's dominance in the computer industry than by an interest in furthering technology.

In these books, young readers will encounter inspiring stories about real people who achieved success despite enormous obstacles. Oprah Winfrey—the most powerful, most watched, and wealthiest woman on television today—spent the first six years of her life in the care of her grandparents while her unwed mother sought work and a better life elsewhere. Her adolescence was colored by pregnancy at age fourteen, rape, and sexual abuse.

Each author documents and supports his or her work with an array of primary and secondary source quotations taken from diaries, letters, speeches, and interviews. All quotes are footnoted to show readers exactly how and where biographers derive their information and provide guidance for further research. The quotations enliven the text by giving readers eyewitness views of the life and accomplishments of each person covered in the People in the News series.

In addition, each book in the series includes photographs, annotated bibliographies, timelines, and comprehensive indexes. For both the casual reader and the student researcher, the People in the News series offers insight into the lives of today's newsmakers—people who shape the way we live, work, and play in the modern age.

Is Today the Day?

On February 3, 2008, Eli Manning was where every aspiring football player hoped to be one day—in a stadium about to play in the Super Bowl, football's most celebrated game. Too busy preparing for the game to notice the boisterous crowd in the stands, Manning quietly went through the same regimen he had followed his whole career. He stretched, he sprinted, he threw footballs. In between, he mentally rehearsed the plays he and his coaches thought would work against one of professional football's most revered teams, the undefeated New England Patriots.

The road to the Super Bowl is always fraught with hardship, but Manning seemed to have endured more than most. Coming from a celebrated football family in Louisiana that includes Manning's father Archie, a Hall of Fame quarterback, and his brother Peyton, an all-star professional quarterback, Manning labored in their shadows. People often introduced Eli as Archie's son or Peyton's brother. Even when he compiled decent statistics playing for the University of Mississippi (Ole Miss), where his father had attained legendary status for his football wizardry, daily reminders and questions about being Archie's son consigned Eli to the background. All he needed do was look at any of the hundreds of speed-limit signs posted on campus limiting vehicles to 18 miles per hour (29kmh)—a number specifically chosen to honor his father, who wore number 18 on his jersey when he played for Ole Miss.

While Manning mentally rehearsed his plays prior to the start of the Super Bowl, his quarterback rival for the game, the acclaimed Tom Brady, warmed up on the other side of

Eli Manning, right, grew up with all-star quarterbacks: brother, Peyton, left, and dad Archie.

the field. Behind Brady's efficient hand, the Patriots had swept through the season and playoffs undefeated, the first squad to register that impressive deed since the 1972 Miami Dolphins, and in the process scored 589 points to set a new professional record. Heavy twelve-point favorites to defeat Manning and his team, the New York Giants, the Patriots supported Brady with a strong running game and a defense that swarmed to the ball. Lightning-fast receivers Randy Moss and Wes Welker split through opposing defenses with alarming ease, and running backs compiled yards behind an offensive line featuring three Pro Bowl players. They had already won the Super Bowl in 2001, 2003, and 2004, and most expected that the Giants would be their fourth victim.

Manning enjoyed weapons of his own. The temperamental wide receiver Plaxico Burress harassed defenders with his long stride and his ability to snare balls most could not reach. Amani Toomer complemented Burress to form a dangerous duo, while running back Brandon Jacobs gained more than 1,000 yards during the regular season. A defense anchored by linemen Justin Tuck, Michael Strahan, and Osi Umenyiora

Eli Manning celebrates with teammate Michael Strahan after winning the Super Bowl in 2008.

disrupted opposing offensives with their mad rushes and tackling abilities.

As Eli Manning waited for the final pregame moments to tick away, he could look back at a decent, if unspectacular, career. After earning a bundle of state and national awards in high school, he quarterbacked the University of Mississippi to winning seasons, but to the dismay of Ole Miss fans, never to a championship contest. Alumni expected a reincarnation of Eli's father, Archie, who single-handedly yanked Mississippi to national prominence in the late 1960s, but the closest Eli came was a handful of second-tier bowl games.

New York Giants fans expected the same when the team acquired Eli in 2004. Hungry for a Super Bowl, they assumed that coming from the same family as Archie and Peyton, now a top-caliber quarterback for the Indianapolis Colts, Eli would soon remedy every ill that plagued the Giants. Manning had performed respectably, although interceptions at times were a problem. His strong arm and calm leadership gained admirers, most of whom expected that Manning would one day blossom into an all-star talent.

As Eli Manning listened to the national anthem before the opening kickoff before 70,000 jubilant fans inside University of Phoenix Stadium in Arizona, he wondered if today would be that day.

Chapter 1

Football Runs in the Family

Born on January 3, 1981, in New Orleans, Louisiana, Eli Nelson Manning enjoyed a happy, carefree childhood, one that took shape from the nurturing demeanor of his parents. His father, Archie, had gained fame as an outstanding football quarterback, first from 1968 to 1971 at the University of Mississippi (Ole Miss) and later in the National Football League (NFL) with the New Orleans Saints. Archie amassed such amazing records while in college that the university retired his number 18 and established it as the speed limit for vehicles on campus.

While at Ole Miss, Archie fell in love with the school's homecoming queen and cheerleader, Olivia. The couple wed shortly after graduating from college and gave birth to three sons— Cooper in 1974, Peyton two years later, and then Eli in 1981. An amazing sports saga was about to begin.

"Whatever Season It Was, We Were Outside"

Archie added to his football prowess with fourteen seasons in the NFL, mainly quarterbacking the New Orleans Saints, who made him the draft's number-two selection in 1971. Cooper and Peyton share memories of rollicking around the Saints' locker room and of tossing footballs on the field while their dad practiced, but Eli was too young to recall Archie's time in the professional ranks.

Eli's dad, Archie, played 14 seasons in the NFL, mostly with the New Orleans Saints.

Archie and Olivia made a determined effort to be loving, caring parents, an attitude that resulted, in part, from a traumatic event that occurred when Archie was twenty years old. The college student came home one day to find his father slumped on the floor, dead from a self-inflicted gunshot wound. Archie later told Peyton that he and Olivia made a conscious effort to let their sons know they loved them because his own father had never said those words to him. As a result Archie ends every phone conversation with his sons by proclaiming his affection.

"You never know when you're talking to one of them on the phone who might be there with them," explains Peyton, "or even if they're in somebody's office or at a meeting or something, because the conversation always ends with: 'I love you, Peyt.' 'I love you, Coop.' 'I love you, Eli.'"[1]

The parents also decided to avoid pushing their sons in any direction or to force their participation in sports. They wanted their children to simply have fun, do the best they could, and grow to be well-adjusted, responsible people. Raising professional football stars was the last thing on their minds.

"One Kiss, That's All"

Eli Manning was not just shy in the classroom and the sports arena. In a family where hugs and kisses were the norm, a young Eli held fast to a rigid rule—no kisses except for Sunday. "Somewhere along the way he made a rule that you could only kiss him on Sunday nights," states his mother. "Our family has always been big on hugs and kisses, but Eli wasn't interested. I mean not at all. Then he finally gave in a little and agreed to Sundays. One kiss, that's all. Good night, good-bye, see you at breakfast."

Quoted in Archie and Peyton Manning, with John Underwood, *Manning*, New York: HarperEntertainment, 2000, p. 160.

"I think my parents did a great job of not putting expectations on us," says Eli. "They wanted us to be ourselves and do whatever we loved to do. If we wanted to be in a band or be in a play or do anything, they were supportive of us." Eli adds, "It's not about trying to live up to any expectations. It's just about being yourself, having fun, and trying to do the best you can do."[2]

Each week the family held "board meetings," during which everyone shared their thoughts on coming events. While Archie and Olivia had the final say, each of the three boys had the chance to state what was on their minds and feel part of the process of running a family.

Of course, being sons of an NFL quarterback meant that sports played a dominant role, not because Archie wished it so but because the three boys loved activity. Football, basketball, and baseball all attracted the Manning boys. "Whatever season it was, we were outside," says Eli. "We weren't into computers, Nintendo, or that kind of stuff. We wanted to be outside."[3] Eli tried to accompany his big brothers at every opportunity, but as the youngest, he was frequently relegated to all-day center (someone snapping the ball to others) or dismissed as a nuisance.

Archie often joined the boys, especially in the hard-nosed contest called Amazing Catches. As the boys raced down the field or in the backyard, Archie tossed a football just beyond their reach, forcing his sons to apply extra effort to snare the pass. Eli and his brothers, being the raucous boys that they were, particularly loved playing this game in the mud and rain.

Their parents tried to convey that no matter the activity, the brothers should have fun and exert full effort. According to Archie, he only purchased sports equipment for birthdays and Christmas when the boys had specific requests, not because he tried to nudge them in any direction. "It wasn't football I was pushing," he says, "it was involvement,"[4] whether playing basketball or the piano.

To show their support, Archie and Olivia attended every sporting event in which their sons participated, an amazing accomplishment considering the diverse interests of three active boys. Only when his NFL schedule took him away from home did Archie miss a contest. The parents withheld the three from organized leagues while they were young as they believed the boys should not be exposed to the pressures of winning too soon. They had witnessed adults ruining games for their youngsters with such insistence, and they wanted their sons to appreciate the games for enjoyment's sake, not for individual honors or another notch in the victory column.

"I Talk When I Have To"

Shortly after Eli's birth in 1981, the Saints traded Archie to the Houston Oilers. He played two seasons with Houston and then finished his career with the Minnesota Vikings, a time that required Archie's absence from home more frequently than when he quarterbacked for his hometown Saints. As a result, Olivia established an especially close bond with Eli. By the time Eli attended high school, his brothers were in college, and Eli and Olivia began eating dinner at a restaurant once a week, where they chatted while enjoying pizza or catfish. Since he no longer had to compete with his older brothers for his mother's time, Eli flourished having Olivia's full attention. "Eli and Olivia are certainly very close," Archie says. "They have that special bond that you see between mamas and their baby boys."[5]

Archie worried about being away from home so much when Eli was young. "The awareness hurt most when I'd come home in January and he'd act like he hardly knew me."[6]

Archie's doubts occurred partly because of Eli's quiet nature. He did not utter his first words until he was almost three years old. The family contends that his first clear word was "ball." When Eli did finally speak, he unleashed a complete sentence asking his parents whose cat had walked nearby.

The issue was not that Eli could not talk, but that he preferred to observe everything around him, form his own conclusions, and speak only when necessary. "I talk when I have to," an adult Eli explains. "Otherwise, I don't bother."[7]

With the personable Cooper and the assertive Peyton grabbing most of the attention, Eli would have had trouble standing out anyway. Laughter filled the family's dinner conversations, but the jokes tumbled from his brothers and dad while Eli and his mom listened.

Learning Perseverance

A reading problem during first grade magnified Manning's shyness. He struggled to such an extent that when the teacher called on students to read out loud, he slumped at his desk in hopes of avoiding her gaze. "As a child, it's embarrassing and frustrating," Manning says. "They call on students to read out loud in class and it's one of those deals where you're praying the whole time that they don't call on you."[8]

He credits his mother with helping him improve. She patiently worked with him at home, calmly enunciating words when he faltered and reassuring him that he would unravel the mystery if only he kept at it. His parents even switched Eli to another school that offered extra tutoring in reading, and before his first year ended he had shown dramatic improvement.

With his father on the road for NFL games, Eli established a strong bond with his mother, Olivia.

The ordeal taught Manning valuable lessons. He gained sympathy for those struggling with problems and a bond with the underdog, the person who was not expected to succeed as well as others. He also observed that, with effort, an individual could overcome obstacles and achieve his goals. These lessons became crucial parts of the emerging Eli.

Like most young boys, Eli worshipped his older brothers. Both Cooper and Peyton followed in their father's footsteps, setting records in nearly every sporting endeavor they tried. Eli engaged in hard-nosed backyard football and basketball contests with his brothers, always coming out on the short end until high school, when he finally defeated Peyton in driveway basketball—with no less than a slam dunk settling the issue. Eli cherished the moment, both because he had finally triumphed over his brother and because he had made Peyton proud of him. "You beat your big brother in anything—and that was the first thing I ever beat him in besides ping pong and pool, it was a big step,"[9] declares Eli.

Diverse Interests

Archie Manning knew that his boys faced enough distractions being the sons of a professional quarterback. To avoid adding to their problems he and Olivia decided to send them to the prestigious and private Isidore Newman School in New Orleans, Louisiana, an institution that placed an emphasis on education and extracurricular activities over varsity sports.

Like every other school, Newman offered varsity athletics, but the institution focused on involvement rather than churning out state champions. Had Archie wanted to push his sons into professional football, he would have sent them instead to nearby John Curtis Christian High School, which racks up state championships and attracts hosts of college scouts from places like the University of Notre Dame and the University of Georgia, but he and Olivia wanted to downplay that angle. If their sons blossomed into stellar athletes, the two would then adopt a more serious approach.

Brotherly Competition

Like the youngest child in many families, Eli Manning often existed in his brothers' shadows, watching the acclaim go to them while he struggled to draw their notice. It was nothing his brothers said to Eli, but a battle waged in his own mind, one in which he quietly measured his feats against theirs. The competition was less severe with Cooper, who played a different position than quarterback, but Peyton proved to be a different story. He compiled such incredible numbers passing the ball at the Isidore Newman School that Eli at times doubted he could ever match his brother's accomplishments.

Eli did not even play tackle football in pads until the eighth grade. Until then he attended a variety of sports camps, where he learned how to properly play football, basketball, and many other activities. By high school he had shown enough skill in football that he made Newman's varsity squad as a freshman. Eli also played on the school's basketball and baseball teams. Love of sports, not pressure to follow their father, drove Eli and his brothers.

A Knack for Quarterback

Manning so impressed his coaches as a freshman that in midseason they named him the starting quarterback. True to form, Manning kept silent about the news for a few days, waiting to inform his parents while eating supper the night before the game. "Looks like I'm going to be starting Friday night,"[10] he muttered between mouthfuls of food to his stunned parents.

Like Peyton had done earlier, Eli starred as a quarterback. In his sophomore year he passed for 2,340 yards and 22 touchdowns, earning all-state honors along the way while leading the team to an 8–2 record and a berth in the state's playoffs.

Eli excelled at football and became starting quarterback for the Newman varsity squad when he was only a freshman.

Manning improved his next year, compiling 2,547 yards and 26 touchdowns and advancing his 9–1 team to the state quarterfinals.

Although happy about their son's success on the gridiron, Archie and Olivia were more pleased that Eli maintained his grades and seemed to be growing into a well-rounded individual. Unlike the more outgoing Cooper and Peyton, who gathered friends wherever they went, Eli played pickup games or attended movies with the same tight circle of buddies.

Love, Discipline, and a Little Rivalry

Eli, as well as his brothers, became such wholesome individuals because their nurturing parents not only supported their endeavors, but also let them know that a rigid set of rules regulated their lives. Archie and Olivia emphasized right from wrong and never allowed their sons to muddle the issues. They instilled a respect for elders and authority figures and let the boys know that there would always be consequences for actions, both good and bad.

One key rule was that no matter where they went, the sons were to let the parents know where they were, even if they had only walked from one friend's home to another's. One time Eli failed to return home after a football game and called his parents the next morning to let them know he had spent the night at a friend's. Eli knew he was in trouble, and when his father asked why he had not called the night before, Eli said he figured they would never allow him to stay overnight. "I'll take the punishment," Eli told Archie. "I just wanted to stay out."[11]

Eli quietly accepted his punishment, just as he coolly handles every issue. Whether he wins or loses a game, Eli maintains the same calm, unruffled manner. Unlike athletes who flaunt their achievements, he does not engage in theatrics or boasting whenever he makes a good play or scores a touchdown. For Eli, it is enough that he and his team have done well. In response to his father's congratulations after tossing five touchdown passes in one game, Eli said, "Aw, I was just having fun."[12]

Gaining his brothers' respect or topping their accomplishments means more. He loves that he ran a faster 40-yard sprint in high school than Peyton, and he took quiet satisfaction in being the first of the three to dunk a basketball in their driveway court. He enjoyed it not because it showcased his talents, but because he gained the notice of his big brothers.

Eli attracted college attention his senior year at Newman, when the team barreled undefeated through the regular season before losing in the state quarterfinals. Now over 6 feet (1.8m) tall and weighing 190 pounds (86kg), Eli could toss an accurate pass while being rushed by opposing linemen or zip the ball across field to the sidelines, a pass Archie claims is the toughest in football and the one that separates the outstanding quarterback from the rest. For his feats Manning was selected to the high school All-America team and named USA Today's Player of the Year in Louisiana. College now beckoned.

Choosing a College

In choosing a college, Eli looked to his brothers for guidance. Both Cooper and Peyton had attracted the attention of football scouts in high school. Cooper held high hopes for a college football career until his senior year at Newman. One day he felt numbness in the fingers of his right hand, an ailment that doctors diagnosed as spinal stenosis, a narrowing of the spinal canal. Because of the diagnosis, Cooper could no longer play football.

Eli's brother, Peyton, shocked people by going to the University of Tennessee instead of Archie's school, Ole Miss.

College recruiters flocked to Peyton, hoping to attract the out-standing quarterback to their school. With Archie's background, most Ole Miss fans assumed Peyton would follow his father to the University of Mississippi, but Peyton shocked Ole Miss loyalists by choosing the University of Tennessee. Some fans blamed Archie for not steering his son in the direction of Ole Miss. Archie received hundreds of hate calls and letters, most labeling him a traitor and worse. The ordeal taxed Archie and Peyton, who describes the communications as "brutal calls. We both got blasted hard by Ole Miss people, and while it hurt me a lot, it hurt mainly because of what it did to my dad. He was devastated."[13]

Eli took note of the turmoil, but when his time came to make a decision, he typically underplayed the emotions. He told his father that he wanted no drama to the process, and that rather than drawing out the recruiting he would make his decision by December of his senior year. Archie and Olivia, who dreamed that their son would attend Mississippi, knew that Eli would assess matters on his own, make up his mind, and inform them at his leisure. Even if they had wanted to, there was no point in their trying to sway him one way or another. Eli would handle things his way.

Eli pared the list of schools from 50 to 3 as December approached—Texas, Virginia, and Ole Miss. Some worried that the pressure of attending the same institution as his father, where Eli would constantly be measured against Archie's nearly unattainable statistics, would be more than he could handle, but he discounted those thoughts. "It never bothered me when I was thinking of schools that this is where my father went, or that it'd be too much pressure," Eli says. "It was so long ago, and the students here might know the name, but they weren't here during the time."[14]

Eli leaned toward Mississippi, especially after David Cutcliffe became the new head coach there just as Eli was deciding which college to attend. Cutcliffe had coached Peyton at the University of Tennessee, where the two forged a tight bond, and Eli admired the mutual respect the two enjoyed. As soon as Cutcliffe obtained the head coach position at Mississippi, he contacted Eli about coming to his father's school. "I called Eli the day I got the job," explains Cutcliffe. "He and I had talked when I was at Tennessee, and he told me he wasn't going to Tennessee. When I got this job, I told him all bets were off. I think that was the first phone call I made."[15]

Following in His Father's Footsteps

Archie never asked Eli what his choice might be. He learned his youngest son's decision after a long day of duck hunting. In a phone call, Eli informed his father that he would attend Mississippi.

Eli held a small press conference at Newman to announce his selection. Although he gained state and national honors as an outstanding quarterback, the question of whether he was as good as his brother tugged at Eli. "I was unsure of myself coming out of high school," Eli says. "I had doubts because of all the things that Peyton had accomplished. I didn't think I was as good as him."[16]

Peyton had no such uncertainty. Underneath Eli's photograph in his Newman yearbook Peyton wrote, "Watch out world, he's the best one."[17]

Chapter 2

Steps Up His Game

In opting to play quarterback, Eli Manning had chosen the most glamorous position on the gridiron. However, he also guaranteed that with every pass he threw, fans and observers would compare him to his father, a legend at the University of Mississippi (Ole Miss), and to his older brother Peyton, a star at the University of Tennessee. One of the roughest parts of being Eli Manning was the struggle to fashion his own identity and prove that he was an outstanding quarterback in his own right.

"Archie's Boy"

Manning faced being compared to his famous father from the moment he stepped on the Mississippi campus. "Ever since he arrived at Ole Miss, fans around the nation have compared the sophomore quarterback to older brother Peyton and father Archie," declared the university's newspaper, the *Daily Mississippian*. "He is heralded as the one to lead the [football team] back to glory."[18]

National publications joined in, trumpeting Manning's promise while casting the immense silhouettes of his father and brother in his way. The *New York Times* stated, "From the juke joints of the Delta to the feed stores of northern Mississippi, he is called Archie's boy, a son of one of sports' most famous Sons of the South. In Tuscaloosa, Ala., in Knoxville, Tenn., and in every other castle in the Southeastern Conference football kingdom, he is Peyton's brother."[19] Nowhere, it seemed, was he just Eli Manning.

In a small sign that he hoped to carve out his own legacy, Manning declined to wear his father's uniform number, #18, when

Eli wanted to create his own legacy at Ole Miss and chose #10 instead of his father's old #18.

the university offered to bring the jersey out of retirement. He did so mainly out of respect for his father's accomplishments, but he also wanted to make his own mark. He settled on #10 instead.

Making His Mark at Ole Miss

Manning posted stellar marks in the classroom, making the dean's list his second semester with an A average while majoring in business, and attracting a tight collection of new friends with his humor and mild demeanor. Nothing seemed to rattle the easygoing Manning, whom friends nicknamed "Easy."

His jovial nature landed him in an awkward spot a few months after arriving at Mississippi when police arrested him for public intoxication and being a minor in possession of alcohol. He was outside his fraternity house during initiation week, drinking a few

Coach Cutcliffe, right, put Manning on a nightly curfew after he was arrested for public intoxication.

beers with his friends, when a police officer drove by. Suspicious of the crowd of beer-toting students standing around, the officer stopped and arrested Manning and a handful of others.

A mortified Manning telephoned his father the next morning to explain the incident. Manning claimed he was not drunk. He told his father the other students had doused him in beer, and after the police officer took one whiff, he was arrested. Archie listened calmly, then told his son that whether or not he had too much to drink to accept his punishment, learn from it, and move on.

Coach David Cutcliffe used the incident to push his quarterback to think about his future. He placed Manning on a nightly curfew for the rest of the year and had a long talk with his player. Cutcliffe told Manning that he had a choice to make—either he was going to be serious about playing football and finishing college or not. He asked Eli to think about it before answering.

Manning replied that he wanted to be a serious quarterback, not one who plays a few games and is quickly forgotten. He left the discussion more determined to study film of football games, work harder in the weight room, and be the leader that the team needed.

Early College Play

At the time Manning attended Ole Miss, college regulations stipulated that an athlete could play on the varsity squad no more than four years during his college career, so Manning was confined to the practice field during his first year at Mississippi. To give a player time to adapt to his new surroundings and to learn the collegiate game, many institutions redshirt freshman athletes. This means that they are restricted to the practice field and do not play in any games. This one-time step allows the athlete to gain experience without losing one year of eligibility, which would occur if the player stepped on the field for even one play during a game.

Coach Cutcliffe redshirted Manning for the fall of 1999, Manning's first year at the university. As the backup quarterback the next year, Manning played in a handful of games, completing 16 of 33 passes for 169 yards. Although Cutcliffe usually inserted him into games that had already been decided, Manning gained

To Play or Not to Play

Coach David Cutcliffe redshirted Eli Manning for the fall of 1999, Manning's first year at the University of Mississippi. Manning's father, Archie, agreed with the decision, but feared that, as the year went by and the media pressure grew to play Eli, the coach might cave in. Archie worried that his son would miss a valuable year learning the college game, while losing one year of eligibility by appearing in only a few games. The anxious father held his breath during the final home game of the season when the team's starting quarterback, Romaro Miller, fell with an injury. Would Cutcliffe play Manning this late in the season? However, after a few moments Miller rose and returned to play. Manning retained his year of eligibility for future use.

valuable experience. While Manning could accomplish much on the practice field, he could only learn what the game was actually like while being a part of it.

The team's record of seven wins and four losses during the regular season earned Mississippi an invitation to play West Virginia University in the Music City Bowl in Nashville, Tennessee. Although not a major New Year's Day contest, the game rewarded Ole Miss for its winning season. Manning did not expect to play much, but he enjoyed the chance to participate in the postseason festivities.

Nothing went right on the field, however, as West Virginia dominated play for three quarters while racing to a 49–16 lead. With an ineffective offense behind starting quarterback Romaro Miller gaining few yards, Coach Cutcliffe inserted Manning, figuring that with victory apparently out of reach, he could at least give his young quarterback experience in a bowl game. If Manning were to be next year's starter as expected, he had to show he could excel in difficult situations.

"I Proved to Myself That I Could Do This"

Manning did more than that. With calm assurance he led his team downfield, capping his first drive with a 23-yard touchdown pass to narrow the gap to 49–23. After the defense halted West Virginia, four minutes later Manning added a second touchdown pass from 18 yards out, and later topped an amazing display with his third score with seven minutes remaining to bring his team within reach at 49–38. A game that West Virginia had all but put in its pocket now seemed in jeopardy, but an interception of a Manning pass ended the threat. Although his team lost, Manning had shown a knack for leading the team in completing 12 of 20 passes for 167 yards and 3 touchdowns.

Manning impressed his coaches and teammates with the solid play. All-American offensive tackle Terrence Metcalf said, "Eli is an intense competitor and an all-in-all good guy. We have a lot of confidence in him because he knows the calls and completely understands the plays."[20]

For the first time as a college football player, Manning had illustrated his ability to compete at that loftier level. He had amassed records by the barrelful in high school, but now he saw that he could perform as capably in college. "It helped me a lot," Manning stated. "I got my first touchdown pass. I got in the groove as I got more and more action. I proved to myself that I could do this. It gave me confidence that I can play quarterback on this level and my teammates gained confidence in me in that I can be a leader and help put points on the scoreboard."[21] He would be able to build on his performance in the bowl game and hopefully return Mississippi to national prominence.

During the off-season, Manning followed a rigorous regimen. When not attending classes to gain his marketing degree, the 6-foot (1.8m), 4-inch (10cm), 212-pound (96kg) quarterback lifted weights with teammates, studied the playbook to better grasp the many different schemes and attacks the offense would use the next year, and scrutinized film of each game to pick up opponents' tendencies and learn from mistakes made.

Cutcliffe liked what he saw in his quarterback as the next season approached. He said,

> Eli is an extremely prepared young man. He has not wasted his first two years here. He's worked hard to make every practice his game. I feel that we are not going out there with a player who is a "true" rookie. I know that we will experience some things along the way, and there will be bumps in the road. My expectations of Eli are for him to compete, to have fun playing his position, and to play his role within the system.[22]

Starting Quarterback

By the time the 2001 season opened on September 1 against Murray State, Manning's first as a starting quarterback in college, a more-polished Manning stood behind the center. Coach Cutcliffe had seen the progress since the Music City Bowl, but had to hold final judgment until Manning had executed his responsibilities over a period of time.

Manning had to study the playbook and gain experience before he could start for Ole Miss.

"Eli has been in our system two years. He's a very prepared football player, but…the last time he started a football game was at Isidore Newman School in New Orleans," Cutcliffe said. "Eli can play really well early, but he just doesn't have games under his belt. Experience is our best teacher, sometimes it's a cruel teacher."[23]

Manning's father understood Cutcliffe's point. Archie claimed that few positions in sports offer the challenges and demand more skill than the quarterback position. Not only must the athlete be able to hurl a football into tight locations, placing the ball for his receivers exactly where it is needed and at precisely the speed required, often while scampering from 300-pound (136kg) lineman trying to crush him, but he also has to exhibit leadership qualities. He has to know his part in each play, as well as understand the roles and skills for his ten teammates and the opposing eleven defenders. This requires someone who wants to be in the middle of the action, especially in close games or in desperate situations, and who wants to be the one mostly responsible for the game's outcome. "The homework alone—watching film, poring over playbooks—is mind-boggling,"[24] explains Archie.

Manning knew that most Ole Miss fans expected him to at least match, if not surpass, what his father had done a generation earlier and what his brother had accomplished just a few short years ago in his college football career. Manning addressed the point before the Murray State game. He preferred that it not be a major issue, but he recognized that the concern would be a fact of life for him. He said, "A lot of people are expecting more because of my father and brother, but you can't worry about that and live up to everybody's expectations. I just got to go out there and be myself, work hard, watch film, practice, and just do my best."[25]

His best turned out to be great. In an opening 49–14 trouncing of their opponent, Manning completed an outstanding 20 of 23 passes for 271 yards and five touchdown passes while leading his team to a win over Murray State University. The next week, against archrival Auburn University, three Manning touchdown passes brought the team back from a 27–0 third-quarter deficit, but time expired before he could add a fourth. Wins over Kentucky and Arkansas State University, both on the road, improved Mississippi's record to 3–1 as they headed for a crucial home clash against one of the nation's toughest squads, the University of Alabama.

"The Drive"

For a decade Alabama's football team dominated Mississippi's, winning ten straight games in the annual contest. The same story seemed about to unfold this time as Alabama jumped out to a 24–14 lead, but Manning and a stiff defense had other ideas. Mississippi's defense held Alabama to 17 yards and no first downs in the fourth quarter, allowing Manning time to work his magic. A touchdown narrowed the gap to 24–20, and when the defense held again, Manning had the ball back on his 41-yard line with time dwindling.

One of those moments ensued that stick in fans' memories and mark a player for greatness. "Coach Cutcliffe told me before the winning touchdown, that this is the position a quarterback wants to be in at the end of each game," said Manning. "You're the one that decides if your team wins or loses. You're in control."[26]

In what Ole Miss followers labeled "The Drive," Manning led his team toward the end zone. On the second down Manning dropped back to pass, deftly eluded three Alabama defenders racing in to tackle him, and heaved a 41-yard pass to his fullback, who lumbered to the Alabama 3-yard line to put the team in great position to snap the losing streak.

Manning goes back to pass during "The Drive"—taking the team 59 yards for a touchdown to beat Alabama in 2001.

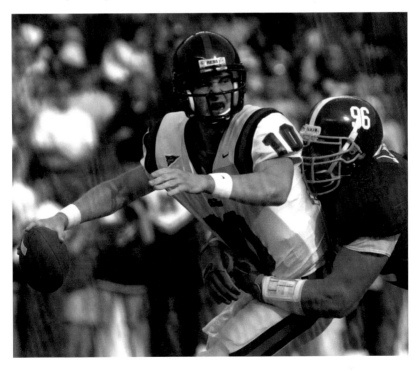

With the student section cheering madly in anticipation of scoring the go-ahead score, Alabama stopped Mississippi's first play. With the clock now under a minute, Manning skirted to the side in an apparent running attempt, but found tailback Joe Gunn short of the goal line. He lobbed an accurate pass to his receiver, who scampered in for the winning score.

Manning exited the field to the cheers of Mississippi followers, taking delight in the dramatic comeback while downplaying his part. "He didn't have much to say," Archie Manning later explained. "He felt good about what he did, but wasn't real excited. He was just Eli."[27] The *New York Times* later reported, "Last Saturday, Eli Manning followed his father into Ole Miss lore by taking the Rebels 59 yards for a last-minute touchdown and an upset of Alabama,"[28] comparing Eli to his father while handing out its compliment.

A Quiet Manner

Coach David Cutcliffe claims that Eli Manning's quiet manner calmed the other players, who followed his example on and off the field. Cutcliffe says,

> He commands respect because he has a great work ethic. In whatever we do, whether it's studying tape, lifting weights or working in the summer program on their own, Eli is always there to set the tempo. His teammates realize the commitment he's made. They understand that he already knows the entire offense, and he is mentally in tune to what we are doing. They respect him so much, and they will follow him. Eli's kind of sneaky about it. He definitely has leadership capabilities. He commands respect in his way, and people like him. He is an easy guy to like.

Quoted in Peter Ross, "Ole Miss' Manning: A Golden Arm and a Sterling Pedigree," *Daily Mississippian*, August 31, 2001, http://www.highbeam.com/doc/1P1-46600277.html.

Manning gained confidence from the stirring victory, following the win with a triumph against Middle Tennessee State University and a three-touchdown performance against another bitter rival, Louisiana State University (LSU). Coach Cutcliffe observed a growing composure in his quarterback, who seemed more comfortable in pressure-packed situations. With his first scoring pass of the game, Manning tied a school record by throwing a touchdown pass in eight consecutive games, a record first set by Mississippi's greatest quarterback—his father.

Manning continued his heroics the next week against University of Arkansas. Tied at the end of the fourth quarter, the game headed into overtime, where each team received the ball on the opponent's 25-yard-line. Both teams scored on the first overtime possession, failed to score on the second, then maintained the tie by pushing across touchdowns in the next four overtime possessions. With excitement mounting, Arkansas scored and added a two-point conversion for a 58–50 lead, meaning that to avoid defeat Manning would have to do the same. He hurled another touchdown pass to bring his team within two, but when the conversion failed Arkansas headed off with a 58–56 victory.

The loss sent the team into a tailspin, as Mississippi lost two of its last three games to end the season with a 7–4 record. Manning was proud of his first year as the starting quarterback. He completed 259 of 408 passes for 2,948 yards, but more impressively, threw 32 touchdown passes while being intercepted only 9 times. However, he labeled the year an overall failure, as under his leadership the team neither captured a conference championship nor received an invitation to a postseason bowl game.

Family Advice and Support

He may have been disappointed in the season overall, but Manning had absorbed much in 2001. He learned that no matter how experienced, a quarterback has good days and bad, and that he must become neither too excited over the positive

Eli has always been able to talk to his brother, Peyton, throughout his career about football and leadership.

performances nor too shaken by the defeats. His father told him to expect harsh criticism with the glory, and that if a quarterback cannot accept the praise for victories and the censure for defeat, he should find another position to play.

Most of all, Manning enjoyed a great tutor in his older brother. He and Peyton chatted each week about the game, about leadership, and about a host of other issues. "Peyton is the one I look up to because I have watched him play and develop in the same system," explains Manning. "I have seen him deal with the pressure of being a college quarterback and the whole process. He has taught me how to read and study film, and I usually talk to him once a week about what brothers talk about. But if I need to ask him a question, I know he understands what I am talking about because he was in the same system."[29]

Chapter 3

Great Expectations

Eli Manning hoped that he could continue to progress in the 2002 season. Football experts expected great things, as they included Manning in their select list of quarterbacks considered hopefuls for college football's highest honor, the Heisman Trophy, awarded each year to the top player in college football. When an inconsistent season unfolded, annoyed fans targeted Manning as the main cause.

Off to a Good Start

Easy victories against the University of Louisiana-Monroe and the University of Memphis, in which Mississippi outscored its opponents 69–19 and Manning tossed three touchdown passes, raised anticipation at Ole Miss, but a tough loss against Texas Tech University brought fans back to earth. Trailing 28–7 at halftime, Manning passed for almost 400 yards and three touchdowns in a furious comeback that fell short, 42–28.

He redeemed himself the next week. Although heavily favored to trounce an ineffective Vanderbilt University, Mississippi's defense collapsed in the fourth quarter and yielded three touchdowns that tied the game with seven minutes remaining. Manning answered by guiding the offense 80 yards for the winning score. The team's record of 3–1 after four games looked better than their play on the field indicated.

The contest against the University of Florida would showcase both the team and Manning, for they faced a nationally ranked team in the Gators, led by another gifted quarterback,

In this big 2002 game against the nationally ranked Florida Gators, Manning helped Ole Miss win 17–14.

Rex Grossman. "This is a big game," stated Manning before the opening kickoff. "Since I've been here, it's probably the best team I've faced so far. It's going to be a big game for us, and it's going to be a challenge for us."[30]

Although Florida vaulted to a 14–2 lead at halftime, Ole Miss's defense intercepted two Grossman passes, giving the ball back to Manning in decent field position both times. The offense, behind their running game, scored fifteen points to win, 17–14. Despite the victory, Manning's erratic production—only 154 yards gained through the air and no touchdown passes, the first time that had occurred in his collegiate career—had some fans questioning his leadership.

He regained form the next week, throwing three touchdown passes in a 52–17 triumph against Arkansas State University. The team's 5–1 record lifted them to twenty-first in the national rankings and built prospects for an appearance in one of the major bowl games, while Manning's performance in the first six games enhanced his chances for the Heisman Trophy.

Heisman Hopes Dashed

A monumental collapse ended both major bowl and Heisman hopes when the team lost the next five games. Manning, who had thrown eleven touchdown passes and only three interceptions in the first six games, saw his production plummet in the five

New York Giants general manager Ernie Accorsi was impressed by Manning's skills and called him "the complete package."

losses to six scoring tosses while being intercepted ten times. The abysmal performances ended Manning's chances of capturing the Heisman Trophy, although he led the 6–6 team to a 27–23 win over University of Nebraska-Lincoln in the Independence Bowl.

The rocky year produced one positive—Manning impressed the New York Giants' general manager, Ernie Accorsi. In November Accorsi attended the Mississippi-Auburn game after hearing good things about Manning. Accorsi warmed to the young quarterback in pregame drills, where Manning displayed a powerful and accurate arm, then watched as Manning repeatedly kept his team in the game. Manning never lost his composure or berated teammates after mistakes, even when Mississippi came up one score short. Despite a 31–24 loss, Accorsi liked that Manning wanted the football in his hands with the game on the line and concluded in his scouting report to the Giants, "I think he's the complete package." Accorsi added that Manning "has courage and poise In my opinion, most of all, he has that quality you can't define. Call it magic."[31] He urged the Giants to draft Manning should the athlete decide to leave school after his junior season.

Faces Choice to Go Pro

The poor season created speculation about whether Manning would leave school for the National Football League (NFL) draft. (The NFL draft is an annual event where the NFL teams select players from the NCAA college system.) He dropped a hint shortly after the season when he said, "I haven't accomplished everything I've wanted to"[32] in college. While he had thrown 31 touchdown passes the previous year against only 9 interceptions, Manning had this junior season seen his touchdowns drop to 20 while his interceptions rose to 15.

Manning discussed the issue with his coach and family. Together with Archie and Peyton, Eli chatted with NFL scouts to determine where in the draft he might be chosen. The big money went to those selected early in the first round, but most analysts expected Manning to go late in the first round, after two other college quarterbacks. They recommended Manning remain at Mississippi and gain another year of valuable experience.

Two simple reasons settled the issue. Manning wanted to conclude his college career with a better season than 2002, and he still enjoyed college life. "I didn't play as well as I wanted to last season," he remarked. "It's a chance to be a captain and leave with the guys you came in with."[33]

"I Wanted to Stay"

A weekend hunting trip with Archie and Peyton, during which the trio discussed the matter, settled things. Eli called Coach Cutcliffe to inform him of his decision to remain, then answered reporters' queries by stating, "It just came down to

Manning wanted to stay at Ole Miss for the 2003 season to gain more experience before heading to the NFL.

'Do you want to go? Or do you want to stay?' And I wanted to stay."[34]

His decision thrilled Ole Miss fans, who hoped their quarterback would rebound with a winning record. His name again appeared among the select list of Heisman candidates.

Manning downplayed preseason optimism about his own play, preferring instead to shift the focus on the team. He asked the university's publicity department not to mount a campaign to promote him for the award, and he preferred to share the cover of the 2003 football guide printed by Mississippi with three teammates and Coach Cutcliffe instead of adorning it himself.

"There's not going to be a campaign, no bobbleheads, nothing like that," said Langston Rogers, the university's sports information director. "We're not even using the H-word. He would be embarrassed."[35]

Individual honors meant little to Manning. He wanted to become a better quarterback and help his team to a winning season. Besides, if he had any illusions of greatness, Peyton was close by with admonitions. "Peyton isn't Eli's older brother so much as he's his second father," explains Cooper. " 'Did you lift today, Eli?' 'Did you work out?' 'You better study hard, now, Eli.' "[36]

Last Season at Ole Miss

A season of hope opened with a 24–21 victory over a Vanderbilt University team that Ole Miss should have handled with ease. The team traveled to Memphis, Tennessee, the next week, where Manning led the offense to six consecutive scores, including four touchdown passes. However, an errant defense combined with two Manning interceptions handed Memphis a 44–34 win.

Manning could barely hide his disappointment over the loss but refused to lose faith in the team. "I know the fans are disappointed," he said after the game. "The team is disappointed. We thought it was a game we should have won, but you can't always worry about fans being disappointed. You have to worry about your teammates. You want to help everyone bounce back and get their confidence again."[37]

Manning exits the field after a loss to the LSU Tigers, but his performance in this game earned the respect of some Heisman voters.

Nervous fans took little comfort over the next two games: an easy victory over the University of Louisiana at Monroe, then the Texas Tech University contest, where Manning compiled more than 400 yards passing in a 49–45 loss. Instead of owning a winning record, the squad languished with an undistinguished 2–2 mark after four games. An ineffective running game and dropped passes were key factors, but Ole Miss fans directed their barbs toward Manning. Shouted references, including "Daddy's boy" and "Mr. Overrated," stung Manning as he ran off the field. Hardest to hear, though, was

"It's Been a Great Run"

Eli Manning experienced highs and lows in his college football career—spectacular wins, bitter losses, fan adulation and condemnation. With his win in the Cotton Bowl, however, he walked away from the University of Mississippi (Ole Miss) on happy terms. Manning relished the victory that closed his career at Ole Miss. He said, "To come to the Cotton Bowl and have your last game with all of those guys and get out a win—that's the most important thing going to a bowl game is to win it—is something I will always remember. It's been a great run."

Quoted in Steven Godfrey, "Rebel Run Culminates with Cotton Bowl Victory," *Daily Mississippian*, January 7, 2004.

when caustic fans harshly compared Eli to his older brother by labeling Eli, "Diet Peyton."

Manning tried to ignore the criticism, preferring to answer his detractors with his play on the field. Using the harsh words as motivation, Manning responded by taking the team to victories in six of the final seven games. The wins included triumphs over the powerhouse team of the University of Florida, which had not lost to an unranked opponent at home in fourteen years; three touchdown passes in a 43–28 win over archrival Alabama and clutch play in the waning moments for a 24–20 defeat of a solid Auburn University squad. The sole loss over that stretch came against Louisiana State University (LSU), ranked third in the country, but Manning kept Ole Miss, ranked fifteenth, in the game until the final moments. With LSU ahead 17–7 in the fourth quarter, Manning tossed a touchdown pass to narrow the gap to 17–14, then took the team into field-goal range with less than four minutes remaining. A missed attempt handed LSU a hard-fought 17–14 win, but with Heisman voters scrutinizing his performances, Manning earned praise for his heroics.

To the Cotton Bowl

A season-ending triumph over Mississippi State University, in which Manning threw three touchdown passes in a 31–0 shellacking, gained the team an invitation to the Cotton Bowl, one of the premier New Year's Day bowl games. In his four years at the University of Mississippi, Manning had broken forty-five school records, yet failed to collect a national championship or even a win in a major bowl. He looked forward to remedying that in the Cotton Bowl and tried not to focus too much on the fact that the last time Ole Miss brought home a New Year's Day victory was in 1970, when his father was the starting quarterback.

In December Manning traveled to New York City for the Heisman Trophy announcement. Despite compiling impressive numbers, Manning placed third in the voting behind University of Oklahoma quarterback Jason White and University of Pittsburgh wide receiver Larry Fitzgerald. Manning matched his father's third place showing in 1970, one notch below Peyton's runner-up status in 1997. Although he failed to take the Heisman Trophy, Manning did receive the Maxwell Award for being the nation's best all-around athlete.

On January 2, 2004, Manning led his team, ranked sixteenth, onto the field in Dallas, Texas, to face a tough foe in Oklahoma State University, ranked twenty-first. He notched two touchdown passes to lift the team to a 17–14 halftime lead, then capped a brilliant 97-yard scoring drive with a quarterback sneak in the third quarter to increase the margin. The defense halted a furious Oklahoma State comeback attempt for a 31–28 win, in which Manning completed 22 of 31 passes for 259 yards and two touchdowns, as well as running for a third. His feats gained Manning the Offensive Player of the Game honors, recognition among Heisman voters, and heightened interest of the National Football League, where analysts named Manning as the NFL draft's likely first selection. Manning's decision to remain at Mississippi another year had paid dividends.

"It was vintage Eli, one last time," declared the campus newspaper. "The last quarterback of the storied Manning legacy ended

Manning threw for 259 yards and 2 touchdowns during the Cotton Bowl, earning Offensive Player of the Game honors.

his career at Ole Miss on a high note"[38] He had taken Mississippi to its first ten-win season in more than three decades and returned with the school's first January bowl victory since his father's 1970 Sugar Bowl triumph.

NFL Draft Controversy

Manning started immediately preparing for the NFL draft by participating in a series of workouts for professional scouts. A nervous Archie could not even be in the building to watch his

"It Was My Decision"

Upset San Diego Chargers fans blamed Eli Manning's family for Manning's reluctance to play in California. Ever protective of his loved ones, Manning made a point of explaining who made the ultimate decision. "It wasn't the Manning family acting; it was my decision," Manning told the press. "My father came out and spoke for me. He was asked questions about it; he got brought into it. San Diego wanted him to come out and visit, to talk to him after we made our decision. It was my decision and it was how I acted; it was my decision that I didn't want to go there. That was the case." Manning tried to deflect criticism of his father by taking sole responsibility and claiming that he simply hoped to play for an organization that offered more promise than he thought the Chargers did. He said, "No, I'm not taking my dad 'off the hook.' He was getting a lot of bad comments. It wasn't my dad; it wasn't my dad's idea; it was my idea. It was my decision to make, and my dad was just supporting me and backing me up, like a father should do. He was getting a lot of bad publicity for doing nothing but backing up his son."

Quoted in Jerry Magee, "Looking Out for No. 1," *San Diego Union-Tribune*, September 21, 2005, www.signonsandiego.com/sports/chargers/20050921-9999-1s21manning1.html.

Manning was disappointed to be picked first in the NFL draft by the San Diego Chargers and was later traded to the New York Giants.

son during the first workout, but after a few plays, a scout told Peyton to inform Archie he had better come inside if he did not want to miss an impressive performance. Eli wowed the professional observers by throwing laser-sharp passes all over the field and displaying an accurate, strong arm.

As draft day approached, most scouts believed the San Diego Chargers would select Manning with the draft's number-one pick. Archie had played his entire career for teams with losing records, and when the family analyzed the Chargers situation, they concluded that Eli would be better off with a different organization. The New York Giants, especially, offered enticements the Chargers lacked—a winning tradition, endorsement possibilities, and the allure of the Big Apple. Manning's announcement that he preferred not to play for the Chargers incurred the anger of Chargers fans, many of whom blamed Archie for swaying his son.

On April 24, 2004, with Eli and his family anxiously waiting to learn his professional fate, the Chargers selected Manning with the first pick. Although he halfheartedly went through the ritual of donning a Chargers cap and holding up a jersey with his name on the back, a disappointed Eli stated he might instead return to school for a law degree.

Lands with the Giants

Events behind the scenes produced a different outcome when the New York Giants, based on glowing reports from their scouts about Manning's potential, arranged a deal with the San Diego Chargers. In the draft the Giants chose quarterback Philip Rivers from North Carolina State University, then promptly traded Rivers and three other draft picks to the Chargers for Eli Manning. "I was walking between interviews," explains Manning, "and a little kid ran into the room and said I had been traded to the Giants. I thought he might be joking with me."[39]

Manning signed a six-year contract with the Giants that, with incentives for outstanding play, stood to earn Manning up to $54 million. Some Giants fans wondered if the team had given up too much to obtain Manning—four draft picks were, after all, quite a bundle—and others argued that the Giants could have retained those picks by selecting another quarterback, Ben Roethlisberger from Miami University in Oxford, Ohio. Skeptical fans remained unconvinced. Manning would have to prove on the field that the Giants had made the right choice in passing on Roethlisberger for Manning.

The Giants could not have been happier. "This is a very special football player," stated Giants coach Tom Coughlin. "Obviously, the pedigree is excellent. His performance in the workouts was outstanding, his accuracy, all his throws, how he carried himself with a certain dignity and class. It was a very exciting thing to witness."[40]

Financially set for life, Manning now had to convince his detractors that he was the real deal.

Chapter 4

Playing in the NFL

Eli Manning expected Giants fans to be critical, but he failed to anticipate the reaction from his new teammates. During training camp rookies are usually subjected to all sorts of pranks, but Manning thought there were other reasons for the pranks being played on him. He earned more money than most of his teammates, he came from a football family, and he replaced two popular quarterbacks. "I don't think someone can really prepare you for what I'm about to go through," said Manning before training camp opened. "I watched his [Peyton's] rookie season, I talked to him as he went through that, and I think it prepares me somewhat, but I think you have to go through it. You have to learn for yourself."[41]

A Hostile Reception

Manning started out on the right foot with his new team. Manning had worn jersey #10 all through college, but punter Jeff Feagles already had that number. When Manning offered to pay for a Florida vacation for Feagles and his family if he would yield the number to Manning, the quarterback impressed other players with his generosity.

The congeniality did not last long. "A guy like Eli will always be judged harshly by his teammates and fans until he proves himself and steps up," said defensive lineman Michael Strahan. "He'll face a hostile environment until he proves he can play. Then we'll welcome him with open arms. If he doesn't, we won't."[42]

Manning, with New York Giants coach Tom Coughlin, left, and Ernie Accorsi, faced a tough situation as most veteran players did not want him in New York.

Manning faced a few issues that other rookies avoided. He came into camp knowing he vied with Kerry Collins, a popular player with his teammates, for the starting quarterback position. Veterans vented their displeasure that a kid out of college might replace an athlete who had already proven his value in the NFL. "He's the guy that's led us to success in the past," said left tackle Luke Petitgout. "For him not to be here would be a great loss." Guard Alan Faneca bluntly declared he preferred the veteran to the Ole Miss graduate. He said, "No, it's not exciting. Do you want to go work with some little young kid who's just out of college?"[43]

Collins created additional turmoil by venting anger over the competition and asking to be traded. The Giants released him and signed in his place a former league Most Valuable Player and Super Bowl winner, Kurt Warner. Other Giants, especially Michael Strahan and star running back Tiki Barber, criticized

Collins's release, claiming they did not want to wait for their chance at championships while a raw quarterback fresh out of college learned how to play.

Fails to Impress at Camp

Conditions intensified once training camp opened. Giants owner Wellington Mara walked by Manning in the dining room and barely knew his quarterback was there. He stated that Manning was "not a guy who jumps out at you."[44] Mara would have preferred his franchise leader to be more outgoing.

Manning's early performances in camp, which led Strahan to compare Manning to a deer frozen in a car's headlights, failed to bolster his image. The outcome paled even more when players recalled that his older brother, Peyton, electrified the Indianapolis Colts from the beginning with his crisp passing and commanding demeanor.

After Manning did poorly at training camp, veteran quarterback Kurt Warner, left, was named the starter.

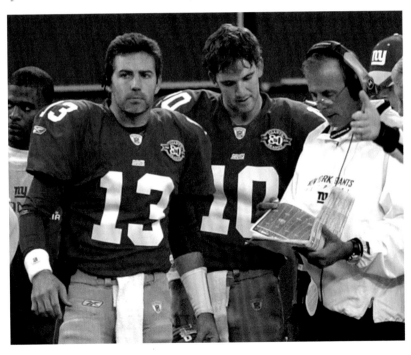

Manning's ineffective preseason, including one game where he completed a mere 4 passes for 20 yards and 2 interceptions, made it easy for Coach Coughlin to hand the starting job to Warner. Warner led the team to a fast start, winning five of the first seven contests and relegating Manning to a backup role. Except for brief action in the season opener against the Philadelphia Eagles, Manning sat on the bench and absorbed as much about the game as he could.

A promising season soured in November, when the Giants lost four straight games and their record dropped to 5–6. With fans clamoring for a look at their new quarterback, and with the team in danger of missing the playoffs, Coughlin decided it was time for a change.

Trial by Fire

Although the team still had a shot at the playoffs, Coughlin switched quarterbacks because he believed Manning represented the Giants' future. He wanted to see how the young player reacted to the pressure of being an NFL starting quarterback. To Warner's credit, the veteran athlete offered to help Manning in any way he could, but other veterans were not as positive. "One of the things guys were upset about during Eli's rookie year was that management seemed to be sacrificing our playoff chances by benching Kurt Warner in favor of accelerating Eli's development," claimed Strahan. Players did not personally dislike Manning, but they wondered how inserting a rookie for a veteran quarterback would help their chance to play in postseason games. "He's an extremely nice kid whom everyone does love personally. But we knew that as a rookie, until Eli stepped up he wasn't ready to lead where we wanted to go."[45]

Manning took over at a precarious time, because in the next five games the Giants faced five of the toughest defenses in the league. If he could post decent numbers and maintain his poise through such severe tests, Manning would be well on his way to convincing fans and teammates that the Giants had not been mistaken in trading for him.

The Professional Playbook

Eli Manning faced a host of adjustments upon entering professional football. None may have been more difficult than the team playbook, a huge collection of rules and plays that each athlete has to know by heart. One page contains the ten steps that Coach Tom Coughlin expects his players to follow simply in breaking the huddle and moving toward the line of scrimmage. Other pages depict running plays, defensive moves, passing schemes, and other detailed material. As a season unfolds, the playbook changes to reflect the next week's opponent, requiring Manning and everyone else to study new material on a weekly basis. Defensive lineman Michael Strahan likened studying the 250-page playbook to preparing for a college entrance exam each week. He said, "The day I retire, I swear I'll never, ever, look at another playbook as long as I live." Strahan admitted its necessity, however, explaining that "football may be a big man's game, but it's also a thinking man's game."

Quoted in Michael Strahan, with Jay Glazer, *Inside the Helmet: Life as a Sunday Afternoon Warrior*, New York: Gotham, 2007, pp. 196, 203.

First Pro Game

On November 21, 2004, Manning led the Giants onto the field for a home contest against the Atlanta Falcons. Fans rose and cheered for the young star, pinning their hopes for a grand future on the leadership, talent, and throwing arm of Eli Manning, but a poor first half dampened their enthusiasm. Manning completed 5 passes for 46 yards and 1 interception as the Falcons built a 14–0 halftime lead. Boos replaced the cheers as Manning headed into the locker room for the break.

In the second half the Giants threatened to score every time they gained the football. Manning tossed his first NFL touchdown pass to

Eli Manning celebrates his first NFL touchdown pass to tight end Jeremy Shockey in 2004.

tight end Jeremy Shockey to narrow the deficit to 14–7, then moved the team into field-goal range in the fourth quarter to pull within four points. With two minutes remaining, Manning trotted onto the field with the chance to lead his team to a game-winning score.

"It's the position you want to be in," Manning said after the game. "As the quarterback you want the ball in your hands with the time running down and you've got a chance to win the game.

That's what it's all about. It's why you play quarterback. It's why you play football."[46]

Manning took the Giants into Falcons territory, but the drive stalled when the team failed to convert on fourth down. Although Manning walked off with a 14–10 defeat, he had impressed his coaches and some of his teammates with his poise and performance. For the game, Manning completed 17 of 37 passes for 162 yards, with 1 touchdown and 2 interceptions.

"You could feel the excitement, the anticipation people had for him, to see what he was going to do, how he was going to be," gushed running back Tiki Barber. "He's going to be our future. But he showed how well he can do this year, not five years from now, but this year." Offensive tackle Luke Petitgout added, "He didn't seem like a rookie to me. He did great."[47]

Manning even convinced the Falcons coach that he had a bright future in the league. "I'm glad we got Eli in his first start and not his fourth or fifth, because he is going to be a tremendous player," said Falcons coach Jim Mora Jr. "I think he's going to be just like his brother in a few years."[48]

Although pleased with his first showing, Manning considered the outing a negative, as he failed to gain a victory for his team. His receivers dropped five passes, but Manning shouldered the blame rather than deflect it to his teammates. "I knew I had to throw the ball better," Manning said. "A lot of times they were bad throws, a little behind them or off to the side. I've got to be more accurate. Sometimes I would throw the ball too quickly." He concluded, "It was disappointing that we didn't win. I made a lot of mistakes. It's a long process."[49]

Making Rookie Mistakes

Tough outings in the next three contests produced an outcry among fans, doubt in teammates' minds, and a determination in Manning to remedy the situation. Against the Baltimore Ravens, featuring a bone-crushing defense, Manning looked like a raw rookie by completing 4 passes in 27 attempts for 27 yards and 2 interceptions, a result that made even Manning's hardiest

A Rocky Start

Eli Manning quickly found out how difficult playing in the National Football League would be. Veteran opponents took advantage of the young quarterback, making Manning look every bit the rookie that he was. Michael Strahan said that Manning looked so confused on the field that some of his teammates "actually started to feel bad for him. Eli was thrown into the fire and took a complete scorching." (Strahan, Glazer) Coach Tom Coughlin offered an equally grim summary: "The young quarterback obviously struggled. He has to stand up and face the fact that he didn't play well. He will have to face his teammates. I expect him to react to this with the hunger to be an outstanding player in this league."(Zillgitt)

Quoted in Michael Strahan, with Jay Glazer, *Inside the Helmet: Life as a Sunday Afternoon Warrior*, New York: Gotham, 2007, p. 137.

Quoted in Jeff Zillgitt, "Giants' Manning Licks His Wounds," *USA Today*, December 12, 2004, www.usatoday.com/sports/columnist/zillgitt/2004-12-12-zillgitt_x.htm.

supporters cringe. Coughlin lifted the young quarterback in the second half, but critics questioned whether Manning had what it took to compete at such a high level.

Ray Lewis, a Ravens linebacker, said they purposely rushed Manning all game to confuse him, and when he looked at the quarterback, he saw "a lot of confusion. You could tell we were really getting to him."[50] Cornerback Deion Sanders accused the entire Giants team of giving up.

Giants teammates agreed with the negative assessments. One told reporters, "We need to go back to Kurt [Warner]. I'm sure guys feel that way. Eli is just shell-shocked. If you're going to develop a young quarterback, then you stick with him. But guys who are fighting their butts off, they want to win now. Guys want the best chance to win now."[51]

As hard as the fans and his teammates were, Manning delivered the harshest statement of what he needed to do. "I'm struggling,"

Manning said. "I know I haven't played well in any of my games. I'm still going to practice and play hard. I know I have to put more into it." He added, "I've got to get my teammates back trusting me. I don't know if I've lost it or not. I haven't proved anything to them."[52]

"He's Going to Get Better"

On the train ride back to New York from Baltimore, Giants quarterback coach Kevin Gilbride saw Manning sitting alone, away from his teammates. When the coach sat down next to his quarterback, the two proceeded to talk the entire trip about what went wrong and how to correct it for the next game. Gilbride told Manning that he had to assert his authority on the field and let his teammates know that he is the boss, that he had confidence in his abilities, and that he would help take them to wins.

Manning and fellow rookie quarterback Ben Roethlisberger played well in a hard-fought 33–30 Steelers win in 2004.

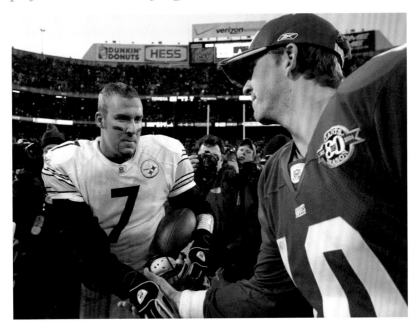

Gilbride believed that part of the problem rested inside Manning's head. Either consciously or subconsciously, Manning was competing with Peyton in the hopes of gaining his big brother's approval. "I think there's something in him that he'd like to show his big brother that 'I'm as big as you are,' or 'I can compete at your level,'"[53] stated Gilbride.

Strengthened by Gilbride's words, the next day Manning walked into Giants Stadium to talk with Coach Coughlin. The head coach was delightfully surprised when Manning, far from being the depressed athlete Coughlin expected, instead talked about leadership and a host of other topics. Manning explained which plays he felt comfortable with and asked Coughlin, who is noted across the league for his complex offensive system, to simplify things. Manning even had a list of plays he hoped the team could focus on in the next few weeks.

Manning had to call on every resource to improve as the next week he and the Giants faced the 12–1 Pittsburgh Steelers. Besides being an archrival, the Steelers were quarterbacked by the athlete critics claimed the Giants should have taken instead of Manning—Ben Roethlisberger. Players and fans alike would be closely scrutinizing every move Manning made, comparing him to the more successful Roethlisberger, who had led his team to eleven consecutive victories.

"If they want to make comparisons, it's fine by me," said Manning during practice the week before the game. "It's the easy thing to do since we both came out in the same year and we're both rookies, but I can't worry about what he's doing. I just have to go out and try to make the best of my situation."[54]

Manning matched Roethlisberger pass for pass in a close contest the following Sunday. Although the Steelers walked off with a hard-fought 33–30 win, Manning gained praise for an improved showing in which he completed 16 of 23 passes for 182 yards and 2 touchdowns. A more confident Manning almost pulled out a win the next week against the Cincinnati Bengals, producing optimism in Giants enthusiasts that their quarterback had found his stride.

"Everyone's really proud of him for hanging in there," said Giants tight end Jeremy Shockey. "He's going to get better, and we've got to get better around him."[55]

A Grand Finale

The positive feelings soared the next week in the season's final game against a strong Dallas Cowboys squad. The Cowboys led 16–7 entering the fourth quarter when Manning went to work. Already notching a touchdown pass in the first half, Manning tossed a second to pull the Giants within two points. When he added a third touchdown pass three minutes later, the Giants leaped into a 24–21 lead. It appeared that Manning might have recorded one of those patented late-game comebacks for which brother Peyton is so acclaimed.

The Cowboys had different ideas, though, as they marched down the field for the go-ahead tally on their next possession. Manning trotted onto the field with less than two minutes remaining, 66 yards between him and the winning touchdown. With a succession of passes intermingled with running plays, he took the Giants to the Cowboys' 3-yard line with sixteen seconds remaining. Coughlin called for a pass, but when Manning stepped to the line of scrimmage and noticed that the Cowboys defense had stacked its players to stop a pass, he switched plays. Shouting an audible—a series of words and numbers indicating to teammates

Manning helped lead the Giants to a comeback win against the Dallas Cowboys in the last game of his rookie season.

the play he was now running—Manning took the snap, handed the ball to running back Tiki Barber, who barreled into the end zone as time expired for the game-winning score.

High Hopes for the New Season

The victory elevated the Giants record to 6–10 on the season. Although disappointing, Manning took heart from the year's final

Father Knows Best

When Eli Manning learned he would start his first professional game, he turned to his father for words of wisdom. As usual, his father did not disappoint. Archie Manning reminded his son that football in the National Football League resembled more of a long-distance race than a sprint, and that he had to avoid getting either too elated with victory or too low with losses. He added that no matter what happened or how he performed, Eli had to go out on the field, do his best, and accept what comes. "I'm going to tell him that you have to be yourself," said Archie. "You roll up your sleeves, you go to work and you just deal with it."

Eli with father Archie in 2005.

Quoted in Ralph Vacchiano, *Eli Manning: The Making of A Quarterback*, New York: Skyhorse, 2008, p. 75.

trio of games, during which he displayed coolness under fire and snatched a last-second triumph from what appeared to be certain defeat. He headed into the off-season with high hopes for the 2005 schedule.

Almost every day Manning lifted weights, ran, studied the playbook, and prepared for the next season. "I've still got a lot to learn," he explained. "I'm going to make mistakes when I see different looks every game. But I think every game I play, I'm going to learn something new and get better. It's just a matter of going out there and trying to get better and taking something from every game."[56]

Manning took advantage of a key asset—his brother. He and Peyton talked frequently about what it meant to be an NFL quarterback, how to determine what the opposing defense intended to do, how to best lead grown men, and how to handle the pressures that come with being a professional quarterback. "It's great that you have a brother and a best friend and a guy who's also the NFL MVP [Most Valuable Player] on your side who you can just talk to,"[57] said Manning.

The 2005 season opened in fine fashion, with Manning adding victories over the Arizona Cardinals and his father's former team, the New Orleans Saints. That set the stage for a road game against the San Diego Chargers, the team—and city—Manning had shunned in the NFL draft. He expected Chargers fans to vent their displeasure at every opportunity.

The Chargers Pour It On

Charges fans did more than vent their displeasure. They wore T-shirts and carried signs bearing critical comments about Manning. One bore the question: "Hey Eli, Will Your Daddy Let You Play Today?" in reference to the belief that Archie had convinced his son to play for the Giants. From the game's opening kickoff, the stadium's announcer made a point of emphasizing Manning's name every time he took the field, producing a cascade of boos from fans each time. The scoreboard displayed "Eli Stats," showing how many incomplete passes he tossed and how often the Chargers defense tackled the quarterback.

Manning, being sacked, was rattled by the San Diego crowd's negativity and boos.

The Chargers responded to their hometown support by racing to a 21–3 lead by the second quarter. A hesitant Manning appeared to be affected by the crowd and rattled by the Chargers defense's string of vicious hits until shortly before halftime, when despite being under intense pressure, he rifled a pass through heavy coverage for a touchdown. The play ignited Manning, who led the team to two more scoring drives to close the gap to 21–20 at halftime.

Manning continued the stellar play in the second half, tossing two touchdown passes and gaining 352 yards in 24 completions for the game in a 45–23 win over the Chargers. Manning showed that he could maintain his composure and execute plays under pressure. "Eli, he's so laid-back, you have no idea," said teammate James Finn, who had also played with Peyton Manning. "You can't tell if Eli's thrown an interception or a touchdown. Peyton, you'll know."[58]

Manning added to his laurels the next week by throwing for a career high four touchdown passes in a 44–24 win over the St. Louis Rams. One New York sportswriter declared that this moment might one day be considered "the dawning of the Eli Manning era, when the switch was flipped on his innate football intelligence and the Giants, after years of futility that stifled the franchise, became an offensive powerhouse."[59]

In winning three of their first four games, the Giants sat as the highest-scoring team in the league behind the hottest quarterback. They had moved on from the miserable season a year ago, when Manning seemed outclassed at times. "It's fascinating to see how he's improved exponentially every week, his decision-making, his comfort level, his ability to get in the huddle and lead us" said running back Tiki Barber. "Especially considering last year, when he struggled mightily. His learning curve was steep. He got pretty intelligent pretty quickly."[60]

Manning's confidence increased in the next few weeks as the Giants captured three of the following four games. At the 2005 season's halfway mark, Manning had guided the team to a 6–2 record and playoff possibilities.

Manning Drops the Ball

All the Giants had to do was maintain the same pace in the season's second half. Although the team performed well in winning five of the final eight games, Manning struggled. He tossed four interceptions in a loss to the Minnesota Vikings, two more in a narrow win over the Dallas Cowboys, and another trio in a win against the Philadelphia Eagles. Had it not been for a stout

The Giants team and its fans had high expectations for Eli Manning.

defense, the Giants would have suffered losses in all three, but as it was, the team kept their playoff hopes alive with two games remaining. All they had to do was win one of the final two contests to enter postseason play.

A loss to the Washington Redskins meant that the season boiled down to one final match—defeat the 4–11 Oakland Raiders and go to the playoffs; lose and miss out. Two big plays—a 95-yard touchdown run by Tiki Barber and a 78-yard scoring pass from Manning to Plaxico Burress—highlighted play as the Giants and Manning rolled to a 30–21 win. With their 11–5 season record, the Giants headed into postseason play.

Unfortunately, in the playoff game against the Carolina Panthers, nothing went right for either Manning or the team as the Panthers waltzed away with a 23–0 shutout of the Giants. In the process they intercepted Manning three times and caused the quarterback to fumble away the ball with a jarring hit. The Giants appreciated that they had made the postseason, but left the game with an uneasy feeling that they had not maintained consistency throughout the year.

The coaches, players, and fans all questioned Manning's abilities. He posted stellar numbers in the season's first eight games, but dropped considerably in the last eight and in the playoffs. Which quarterback would appear in training camp—the athlete with a laserlike throwing arm who confidently guided the team to victory, or the fumbling youngster? After throwing 20 touchdown passes and 10 interceptions in the Giants' first eleven games, Manning tossed only 4 touchdown passes against 10 interceptions in the final six.

Matters worsened for Manning when Ben Roethlisberger took the Pittsburgh Steelers to a Super Bowl triumph over the Seattle Seahawks. Not only did Manning face high expectations from Giants fans and comparisons with his brother, but now Roethlisberger, the quarterback that critics suggested the Giants should have taken over Manning, had also pocketed a Super Bowl victory. When, people wondered, would Eli Manning do the same?

Manning shrugged off the speculations and prepared for the next year. "I didn't play as well as I know I can," Manning said of his season. "I'm going to get better. I know I am. I'm going to be a better quarterback, and I'm going to work hard, and I'm going to do everything I can do to become a guy who can be a leader of this team, and when things aren't going well, take over and get things going. That's where I want to be next year."[61]

Impatient Giants fans expected as much.

Chapter 5

Time to Prove Himself

Football observers expected that the 2006 season would be crucial in Eli Manning's development. Normally a professional quarterback requires at least two years to break into the league and learn what he needs so that he can become the leader that everyone hopes he can be. Would Manning experience a breakout year, or would he fade to the second tier of quarterbacks who register a handful of impressive outings amidst a host of undistinguished performances?

Taking Charge

Manning used the off-season to improve his technique and prepare for the coming year. He studied tapes of every play from the previous season and watched opposing defenses to learn what worked and what failed. He looked at the routes his receivers ran to pick up individual tendencies, such as whether a player favored catching the ball to his right or left side as he ran.

More importantly, Manning decided that he had to be more commanding with the team. He concluded that he had been too hesitant to question the other players, especially those who had more experience in the league than he did. "This year I know what I want," he explained during training camp. "I feel more comfortable taking control of the huddle and correcting someone if they've done something wrong."[62]

Manning used the preseason game in Baltimore, Maryland, to make his point. During warm-ups the normally calm Manning screamed at teammates about being a unified squad and working toward a common goal. The more assertive approach made an impact on wide receiver Plaxico Burress, who liked the take-charge attitude from his quarterback. "You kind of want to see that from your quarterback a little bit, because it kind of gets everybody else riled up," Burress said. "You say, 'O.K., let's go play. Let's go make some plays for the guy.' He's trying to get us excited, get us into the game, and when you have a guy like that, who's a leader of the team, you can't do anything but support him."[63]

Manning had a ways to go before convincing his detractors that he was more than a pale imitation of Peyton or a poor rival to Ben Roethlisberger. "Why can't Eli be like Ben?" asked former NFL quarterback and current television analyst Joe Theismann. "You can't avoid it."[64]

The Manning Bowl

As if he did not already face enough pressure to perform, the regular season's first contest pitted Manning against his brother, the first time in NFL history that brothers took the field as opposing quarterbacks. Reporters labeled the affair the Manning Bowl, and peppered Manning with a host of questions during training camp. Manning looked forward to competing with his brother, but also was eager to get the game over with and move on to the rest of the schedule.

No matter what he did or said, Eli accepted that he would be compared to Peyton. He told reporters that he was not playing against Peyton Manning, but the Indianapolis Colts defense. He could do little to control what his brother did, but he could impact the way the Giants offense performed against the Colts defense. "I'm going to be compared to him. There are similarities and differences. I guess I've just accepted it."[65]

He may have accepted it, but the fact remained that for his whole life Eli had played in the shadow of a family member—first his father and then Peyton. It would take a monumental deed

Called "The Manning Bowl", Eli faced his brother's Indianapolis Colts in September 2006. It was the first time in NFL history that brothers were opposing quarterbacks.

to make his own mark. Michael Strahan noticed the pressure Manning was facing and made a point to tell his quarterback before the game, "Young buck, go out and have some fun."[66]

He did, tossing two touchdown passes and completing twenty passes as he and his brother traded scoring drives. With the Colts holding on to a slim 23–21 lead with five minutes remaining, Eli and the Giants took over at their own 10-yard-line. If he could muster enough plays and drive downfield for a score, Eli would defeat his brother in the same trademark fashion that marked Peyton's play—bringing his team from behind in a last-minute victory. The Colts ended his dreams, however, with an interception of an errant pass. Peyton walked off with the victory, but gushed about his little brother's performance: "It was kind of neat to be on the same field as him, knowing that's my little brother out there." He added, "I told him I loved him. I enjoyed watching him play in person. He's every bit as good as he looked on TV. He's going to be a great player in this league for a long time. I'm proud to be related to the guy. I'm proud to be his brother."[67]

Eli vs. Peyton

In September 2006 Eli Manning and Peyton Manning played against each other for the first time in a NFL game. Nicknamed the Manning Bowl, the game between the Giants and the Colts posed an interesting problem for the rest of the Manning family. "We're just going to deal with it," Archie Manning said. "It was inevitable it was going to happen. I think Olivia and Cooper and the rest of our family look at it as—it's pretty neat. It's an honor to have two of them playing." Archie added that his sons would handle the game as normally as possible. "I know those two guys are going to low-key it. They know they're playing a team sport and they've always done that. We're looking at it that way, too, so we don't want too much attention. We're just going to get through it and hope for a whole lot of offense that night."

Quoted in Michael Eisen, "Archie Shares Thoughts on Manning Bowl," Giants.com, May 12, 2006, www.giants.com/news/headlines/story.asp?story_id=15577.

"He Has Something Special"

Despite the loss to the Colts, Manning impressed Coach Tom Coughlin with his calm direction of the Giants. He added to his luster the next week in a road game against their bitter rival, the Philadelphia Eagles, whose unrelenting defense swarmed on Manning to force him out of his game plan. Rather than following his coach's carefully scripted plays, Manning had to constantly switch calls at the line of scrimmage when he saw how the Eagles had lined up.

The bruising defense sacked Manning eight times as the Eagles built a 24–7 lead going into the final quarter, but Manning took charge and bounced back. Two quick Giants scores, including a touchdown pass by Manning, brought the Giants within three points, but they still trailed as the clock ticked down to less than one minute. Manning's crisp passing moved the team downfield,

The Eagles celebrate after running a Manning interception back for a touchdown. Manning drew criticism for his frequent turnovers and inconsistent play.

where a field goal took the teams into overtime. Manning continued his dazzling play by tossing the game-winning touchdown pass to Plaxico Burress. In the 30–24 victory, Manning completed 31 of 43 passes for almost 400 yards and 3 touchdowns. More importantly, he had displayed toughness in absorbing those repeated hits, in smoothly moving from the playbook to improvised calls, and in gaining that last-minute victory he barely missed against Peyton's Colts.

"Now, he's really showing his maturation," said guard Chris Snee. Even Burress was impressed. "You can never really get him flustered," he said. "That's what I like about him. Some of the plays that he's been making in close games, he's just showing us that he has something special."[68]

Manning experienced a setback the next week by throwing three interceptions—the most glaring weakness in his arsenal—in a 42–30 loss to the Seattle Seahawks, but rebounded with five consecutive wins. At midseason Manning had positioned the Giants for a run at another playoff spot.

More Disappointments

Little went right in the season's second half, when the Giants lost six of their final eight games. Even though they squeaked into the playoffs with an 8–8 record, few took heart in their weak performances. Manning at times appeared confused and hesitant.

Titans' Pacman Jones catches his second interception from Manning in November 2006. The turnover cost the Giants the game.

Especially cruel was the loss to the Tennessee Titans, one of the weaker squads in the NFL. Despite a 21–0 halftime lead, the Giants collapsed and surrendered the lead in the second half. Two critical Manning interceptions helped the Titans roar to a 24–21 victory that left a distraught Coach Coughlin nearly speechless.

The Giants held a team meeting following the bitter loss in an attempt to figure out what went wrong. Manning, who took pride in the study and effort he put into each game, was stunned to hear some teammates admit they failed to properly study the playbook and adequately prepare. Manning had willingly accepted criticism from fans as part of being a quarterback, but now he found that some of the men he relied on were not doing their jobs. Manning turned to backup quarterback Tim Hasselbeck and said, "I'm fighting my butt off and trying to do everything I can, people in the city are calling me a bust and all these things, and we've got people doing this?"[69]

He had an opportunity to start things in a positive direction if he could grab a win in the playoffs. Their first-round opponent, the Philadelphia Eagles, had always provided a stern test for the Giants, and observers concluded Manning's performance could mean the difference between a long off-season and one filled with optimism. "This game right here, how he plays, will determine how much heat he takes during the off-season,"[70] explained Hasselbeck.

Manning dominated the game's first drive, tossing darts to his receivers and lifting his team to a 7–0 lead with a touchdown pass to Burress. In a seesaw affair, the Eagles and Giants traded scores into the final quarter, when the Eagles held a 20–13 lead, but Manning mounted a flawless drive that culminated in another scoring pass to Burress to knot the score. With less than five minutes remaining, however, the Eagles moved downfield and kicked the game-winning field goal as time expired.

Manning played well but walked off another disappointing postseason defeat. Fans who had negatively compared him to Ben Roethlisberger gained added fuel when the San Diego Chargers, the team Manning passed on, compiled a 14–2 record behind the players the Giants traded to obtain Manning. "I've made some strides. I've played well at times and haven't at others," said Manning, who added, "I have to just continue to improve."[71]

As Manning reexamined his leadership role, Peyton delivered another reason for Eli to be the best quarterback he could be. In Super Bowl XLI, Peyton Manning led the Colts to a 29–17 victory over the Chicago Bears, capturing the game's Most Valuable Player award for his heroics. Eli watched his brother with pride, a touch of envy, and a determination to match his brother's accomplishment.

"I know how hard he's worked, how much he's wanted this and what he's put forth to get it," said Manning. "When it comes time for next year, I'll know what that feeling is and know that

A Kid at Heart

Sometimes Eli Manning had to abandon the day's game plan and improvise his tactics on the field, much like youngsters competing in a backyard or playground contest. Although it occurred infrequently, he enjoyed returning to his roots, almost as if he were challenging his brothers in backyard football. Manning says,

> When you're down, you're on the line of scrimmage, you're calling plays, a lot of times you're just kind of—not making things up, you're kind of just playing football. Everything's not perfect, but you're scrambling around and you're doing things that you've never really practiced, and you're still getting everybody on the same page, getting organized. Yeah, it's fun to do sometimes. Obviously it's not what you want to happen; you don't want to be down. You like to have a great game plan and go and execute it the way it's supposed to be done. But sometimes you've got to get off the track and just kind of go play ball.

Quoted in John Branch, "Manning Doesn't Lose His Cool During the Giants' Comeback," *New York Times*, September 19, 2006, www.nytimes.com/2006/09/19/sports/football/19giants.html.

I don't want to be shaking hands and have people congratulate me about Peyton and what he's doing. I want to be in the hotel studying film and getting ready to play for a championship." He added, "Seeing the grin on his face, his smile after the game, and the relief and enjoyment he had put something in my heart that said 'This is where you want to be.' It definitely sparked something with me. It definitely made me want it even more."[72]

The Worst Criticism Yet

In his final twelve games, Manning threw almost as many interceptions as touchdowns. While he posted some great numbers in a handful of wins, Manning looked out of step in some games. Team co-owner John Mara talked with Manning about his need to play more consistently, and fans filled sports radio shows with angry comments about the Giants' future. Criticism became so vicious that one Giants coach, Chris Palmer, said, "You know, I'm sure there are players in the locker room who've said, 'Boy I'm glad I'm not Eli, because I don't know if I could take that abuse.'"[73]

Archie Manning watched his son endure the criticism. As proud as he was with Eli's prowess on the gridiron, Archie was prouder of how his son so gracefully handled fans and sports commentators. "A blitz may get him or some coverage may get him, but the media and the fans aren't going to get him," Archie Manning said. "I'm telling you, they're not going to get him. I'm proud of him, he handles it."[74]

Giants coaches intended to help their quarterback grow into his role. Coach Gilbride talked to Manning about the need to break out from Peyton's shadow and assume his own identity on the football field. He stated that the other players had to see that Eli believed in himself and acted with a reassurance that comes with confidence. Gilbride explained, "You may be the little brother of the Manning family, but you're our big brother here." He added,

Every one of these guys needs to know that you're the guy, you're the leader. You're not the little brother here. You're the guy everyone is looking to, and when things are not going well they need to see a toughness about you, a determination about you that there's no questioning you're going to get this done.[75]

After retiring from the Giants, Tiki Barber took jabs at Manning, questioning his ability to be a leader. Manning fired back, earning the respect of his teammates.

Running back Tiki Barber, who retired after the season, added pressure by claiming during a nationally televised preseason football game that Manning's quiet demeanor negated any chances of him becoming the team leader. He wondered if the players listened to what he said.

Manning waited until he had seen a tape of the interview before replying. To a gathering of reporters, who expected the typical calm statement, Manning ripped into Barber's criticism as the rantings of a man trying to gain favor with a television audience. Manning added that Barber's well-known desire to retire the previous year caused him to lose heart for the game, and that his retirement most likely helped the team. The only people more surprised about Manning's tough response than the reporters were his current teammates, who gained a newfound respect for the quarterback. Gilbride's words and Barber's taunts prodded Manning into taking a more forceful approach.

"Eli the Terrible"

Although the 2007 season opened with a 45–35 loss to the Dallas Cowboys, Manning's four touchdown passes gained notice. He had been the perfect quarterback, masterminding time-consuming drives by mixing running plays with short tosses to his receivers. However, his production dropped in the next seven games. Despite registering a 6–2 record, Manning delivered only another eight touchdown passes along with seven interceptions, his major weakness.

Still, at midseason the team appeared likely to gain a playoff spot. A loss to the Dallas Cowboys and a victory over the Detroit Lions led to a crucial contest against the Minnesota Vikings. With Peyton enjoying a week off and watching from the crowd, Eli experienced one of his worst days. The Vikings intercepted four passes, returning three for scores, and trounced the Giants, 41–17. Irate fans booed Manning off the field, set fire to a Manning jersey, and vented their anger on sports radio shows. The *New York Daily Tribune* labeled him "Eli the Terrible," while Giants management feared Manning might never be the leader

Irate Giants fans booed Manning off the field after he threw four interceptions against the Minnesota Vikings.

they hoped he was when they traded for him. One football analyst thought Manning lost focus and looked timid, while Coach Coughlin disgustedly remarked that a quarterback could not just hand the opponent a victory as Manning had with his poor passing day. With a 7–4 record, though, the team remained in the playoff picture.

Manning continued his roller-coaster year the next week against the Chicago Bears. With the offense sputtering, Manning finally drove the team to the Bears 1-yard line, only to have his pass intercepted. Then, trailing 16–7 late in the fourth quarter, Manning tossed a touchdown to Amani Toomer. He waited on the sidelines while his defensive teammates forced the Bears to punt, then headed onto the field 77 yards away from the end zone with under five minutes remaining. Forgetting the earlier end zone interception, Manning coolly guided the Giants the distance for the winning score. Peyton later stated that "it really stood out how he kind of stayed tough and put the previous plays behind him. I think that's one of the most important characteristics of a quarterback—to put the previous play behind you, good or bad."[76] Peyton later told his dad that what most impressed him about Eli was the guts he had to forget about lapses and focus on what needed to be done.

Adversity accompanied Manning in the final games, however. In a loss to the Washington Redskins, fans booed Manning off the field after he threw thirty-five errant passes, the most incompletions in the NFL in forty years. A victory on the road against the Buffalo Bills—their seventh consecutive victory away from the critical New York fans—gained the Giants a spot in the playoffs, but questions lingered about Manning's effectiveness. His old shortcoming—interceptions—kept appearing when the team least needed it. Still, they headed into their final game with a 10–5 record.

No one expected them to emerge with a victory in the final game, as it came against one of the most-talented squads in NFL history. At 15–0, the New England Patriots, behind star quarterback Tom Brady, had hopes of becoming the first undefeated team since the 1972 Miami Dolphins. Already assured of a playoff spot, the Giants could have rested some of their starting players, but everyone wanted a shot at stopping Brady and the Patriots.

Behind two Manning touchdown passes, the Giants held a 21–16 halftime lead. He and Brady put on clinics, completing passes and compiling yards in a high-scoring affair. Even though the Patriots walked off with a 38–35 win, Manning registered one of his best days. Against one of the league's toughest defenses, Manning completed 22 of 32 passes for 251 yards and 4 touchdowns. He had taken the field against the league's premier quarterback and held his own, a performance that bolstered his confidence heading into the playoffs.

Could he continue the momentum in postseason play? His big brother had pointed the way the year before, in the process enlarging the shadow that enveloped Eli Manning. If he wanted to emerge from that shadow, he had to mount his own drive and win his own big game.

Chapter 6

"The Best Is Yet to Come"

Although Eli Manning had enjoyed a decent career with the Giants, he had failed to fulfill fan expectations and even the hopes of management. If he were to dispel those doubts, he had to show that he could lead the team to the ultimate goal—the Super Bowl. In doing so he would convince both the detractors who loved to attack him and himself that he had forged his own identity, an identity apart from his father and his brother.

The Playoffs Begin

Most sports teams prefer to play their games at home, because they often play better in their own stadium where they have the support of their fan base. The Giants, however, posted amazing numbers on the road, winning seven of eight games, while losing five of eight games in their home stadium. Some wondered if Manning felt more relaxed away from the biting criticism of Giants fans. If so, that could work to the team's benefit because in order to play in the Super Bowl, they would have to win three playoff games on the road.

The team traveled to Tampa Bay, Florida, for the first playoff contest. The Tampa Bay Buccaneers' solid defensive unit planned to take advantage of Manning's tendency to throw interceptions at key moments by applying unrelenting pressure on the quarterback, but Manning adapted. Rather than sit in the pocket and

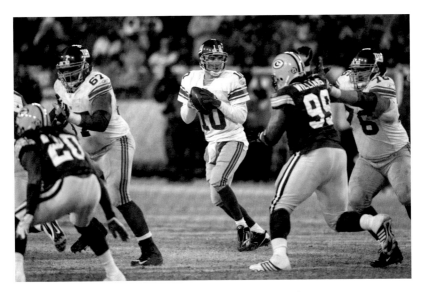

The Giants beat the Green Bay Packers in freezing conditions to claim the NFC Championship.

wait for his receivers to race downfield, he turned to short, quick passes to gain yards. The Giants walked off with a 24–14 victory, Manning's first playoff win.

That set the stage for their second-round game against the Dallas Cowboys, a team that had defeated the Giants twice during the regular season. This was Manning's day, though, defined especially by two impressive drives where he methodically marched the team downfield for touchdowns. A key drive to end the first half, in which Manning tied the score with seven seconds remaining, handed the Giants an emotional boost that carried over to the second half. The Giants notched a 21–17 win for their ninth consecutive road victory, the second straight playoff game in which Manning avoided throwing an interception.

The next game would be no simple affair. They traveled to Green Bay, Wisconsin, to face the heavily favored Packers and their Hall of Fame quarterback, Brett Favre, in a game staged in horrible weather. A biting cold dropped the wind chill to –24°F (–31°C) and forced the Giants to use heated benches, hand gel to warm the skin, and sheepskin to line the inside of their helmets.

Not surprisingly, the game featured numerous fumbles as runners had difficulty holding onto the ball in the frigid conditions. In the fourth quarter, with the game tied, Manning stepped up his play. With twelve minutes remaining he drove the team into field-goal range, but kicker Lawrence Tynes missed a 43-yard attempt. Manning got the ball back with two minutes remaining and again led the Giants into field-goal territory. With four seconds left, Manning spiked the football to stop the clock. All the Giants needed to reach the Super Bowl was a successful field goal, but again Tynes launched an errant kick, this time from 36 yards.

A disappointed Giants team regrouped for overtime, a risky affair in which a mistake or ill fortune often determines the outcome. The Giants defense rose to the challenge, intercepting a Brett Favre pass and putting the ball in Manning's hands. For the third time in less than a quarter's play, Manning guided the offense into Packers territory. As teammates watched from the sidelines, Tynes connected on a 47-yard field goal for a 23–20 win and an entry into the Super Bowl.

Manning had put things together at just the right time. Over the last four games Manning played three of the best teams in the league, including the undefeated New England Patriots, and tossed only a single interception—none during the playoffs—while throwing eight touchdown passes. His greatest challenge, though, lay ahead. Tom Brady and the New England Patriots loomed.

Manning's Ascension

"Oh, brother! Eli, the baby of the Manning quarterback clan, finally has arrived,"[77] declared the Associated Press of Manning's ascension to the Super Bowl. That feat would have been deemed impossible only two months earlier, when Manning's interceptions provoked fan uproar and caused some teammates to doubt his leadership. Faced with the adversity, Manning replied in the only way he could—not with words, but with actions on the field.

Manning faced pro-bowl quarterback Tom Brady and the Patriots in Super Bowl XLII on February 3, 2008.

He faced incredible obstacles, though. Behind Tom Brady, the Patriots had run over every opponent to compile an amazing 18–0 record, and the team already boasted three Super Bowl victories in the past six years. Oddsmakers posted the Giants as 12-point underdogs for Super Bowl XLII, held on February 3, 2008, in Phoenix, Arizona, but the team arrived filled with optimism.

They had almost defeated the Patriots a few weeks earlier, and Manning's stellar play inspired everyone. Although the brash Plaxico Burress predicted a 23–17 victory, Manning took a calmer approach. "We haven't been given a shot, but we're here and I think we're deserving of it. Right now I'm excited as I can be."[78]

Peyton took a hands-off approach. When a reporter asked what advice he would give his younger brother, Peyton referred to the three consecutive playoff victories Eli had just posted and replied, "He doesn't need to hear any advice from me."[79]

Super Bowl XLII

The game started in promising fashion. Completing five of seven passes mixed in with nine rushing plays, Manning led the Giants to a field goal on their first possession in a drive that consumed ten minutes. Not only had Manning given his team the early lead, but he had also kept the dangerous Tom Brady and the potent Patriots offense off the field for much of the first quarter.

New England answered with a touchdown to take a 7–3 lead. Again the Giants offense ground out yards behind an effective combination of running and short passes, but the drive fizzled 14 yards shy of a score when Manning tossed an interception. The game turned into a defensive standstill, and the first half ended with Manning and the Giants trailing by the same score.

Neither team scored in the third quarter. The Giants defense, behind defensive end Justin Tuck, swarmed all over Tom Brady, chasing him out of the pocket numerous times, forcing him into hurried throws, and sacking the quarterback five times.

Manning took over in the fourth quarter, connecting on a 45-yard completion to tight end Kevin Boss and seventeen more to Steve Smith before hitting David Tyree with a 5-yard scoring pass. With eleven minutes left in the Super Bowl, Manning and the Giants held onto a slim 10–7 lead.

Another stout effort by the defense gave Manning the ball. He dropped back to pass, spotted Plaxico Burress wide open, and lofted what looked to be an apparent touchdown pass wide of its mark. Had he been able to make the play, the Giants would

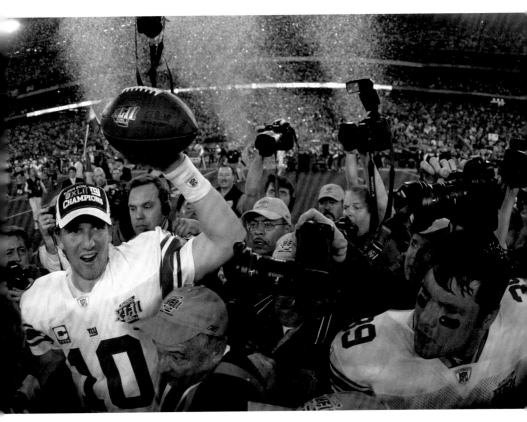

Manning led the Giants in a hard fought game before they won the Super Bowl.

have taken a near insurmountable ten-point lead. A fan sitting near Ernie Accorsi, the scout who urged the Giants to pursue Manning, turned and muttered, "Your quarterback just cost us the world championship."[80]

The fan's gloomy prediction seemed to materialize a few moments later when Brady showed a worldwide audience why he was the most feared quarterback in the league. Completing 8 passes for 71 yards, he led the Patriots on a 12-play, 80-yard scoring drive to give the Patriots a 14–10 lead with only two minutes and forty-two seconds left in the game. In the press box, the nation's reporters began handing in their ballots for the games Most Valuable Player, some selecting Brady and others selecting Patriots wide receiver Wes Welker.

Manning had less than three minutes to bring his team back. He faced the situation he and Peyton had imagined in their backyard football games, where they had the ball in the final moments of the Super Bowl with the outcome on the line. A field goal would do nothing but draw the Giants within one point, so it was do or die for Manning. Either he led his team to a touchdown and a Super Bowl victory, or he headed home for a long off-season.

Manning later explained that he had discussed this situation with his brother, and both agreed that they preferred needing a touchdown to win over having the option to kick a field goal for a tie and sending the game into overtime. "You like being down four when you know you have to score a touchdown to win the Super Bowl," said Eli. "You can't write a better script."[81] Kids everywhere dream of such a spot.

"Let's Go Win This Thing"

In the stands, Ernie Accorsi could barely watch. The quarterback he so strongly recommended now faced the ultimate situation, the one that determined whether a quarterback headed into the

Plaxico Burress catches the game-winning touchdown from Manning with less than a minute left.

The Great Escape

In the 2008 Super Bowl against the New England Patriots, Eli Manning barely evaded being tackled for a loss during a play labeled by reporters as the "Great Escape." Had the Patriots downed him, Manning and the Giants would have lost the game, but he somehow eluded his foes and launched the pass. Teammate Michael Strahan claims that play "took a few years off my life." Referee Michael Carey says he was bringing the whistle to his mouth to stop the play when Manning launched the ball. Carey recalls, "It was like a scene out of *Planet Earth* or *National Geographic*, where it's a lion jumping on the back of a wild horse. You could see him just desperately trying to pull out and somehow he did."

Quoted in Ralph Vacchiano, *Eli Manning: The Making of A Quarterback*, New York: Skyhorse, 2008, pp. 257, 260.

record books as an outstanding leader, or slipped to the back pages as another in the long line of decent athletes who never reached their potential. "You know what?" Accorsi said to his son as Manning took the field. "If he's what we thought he was going to be, he's got to do it now."[82]

Accorsi would have been reassured had he been able to hear Manning's words. As he trotted up to the huddle, Manning stated confidently, "Let's go win this thing. Who's with me?"[83]

With the clock running down and 83 yards separating him from the end zone, Manning hit Amani Toomer for 11 yards. The Patriots held the Giants to no gains in the next two plays, and a Manning to Toomer pass left the Giants inches short of a first down with ninety-four seconds left in the game. If they failed to gain a first down on the next play, the Patriots would take over and run out the clock, so somehow Manning had to squeeze out a gain. With the Patriots guarding against a short pass, Manning called a running play that made the first down by inches. He and the Giants retained the ball.

Then occurred the play that reporters labeled the "Great Escape." With the ball on his own 44-yard line on third down, Manning dropped back. Correctly figuring a pass, the Patriots defenders rushed through the Giants offensive line in pursuit of Manning, who had to race out of the pocket to avoid being tackled. Three Patriots converged on Manning and had the quarterback in their grasp, but moments before the referee whistled the play dead, Manning heaved a long desperation pass to David Tyree. The receiver leaped between two Patriots defenders to snare the pass and fell to the Patriots' 24-yard line. By the slimmest of margins Manning, never known for his running, had kept his team in the game.

Watching from a luxury box at the stadium, Peyton pumped his fist, screamed, paced back and forth, and turned away in torment as his brother kept the Giants' hopes alive. Friends watching on television saw how nervous Peyton was and sent voicemail messages to calm down. On the sidelines, Michael Strahan walked to every teammate telling each that Manning would lead them to victory and that the final score would be 17–14. "I kept telling them, 'Repeat it.' I was walking up the sidelines saying, 'You say it. Repeat it. You have to believe it.'"[84]

A sack of Manning by the Patriots and an incomplete pass left the Giants with a long third down situation, but Manning delivered again by hitting Steve Smith for a first down. Smith immediately stepped out of bounds on the Patriots' 13-yard line to halt the clock.

Only thirty-nine seconds remained. Four Giants receivers sprinted toward the end zone as six Patriots defenders rushed Manning. The quarterback, who had been blitzed throughout the game, counted on the Patriots doing precisely that. Instead of running to either side he quickly lofted the ball toward the left corner of the end zone, where Plaxico Burress snared the pass for the go-ahead touchdown. Manning was half a minute away from a Super Bowl victory and the vindication it brought—vindication as a quarterback, as a star in his own right, as a Manning son and brother.

Tom Brady's reputation for last-minute heroics did not permit the Giants to breathe easy, but Justin Tuck and the defense did not allow a yard. After an incomplete pass, the defense tackled Brady for a 10-yard loss before batting down two more passes to seal the win. As time expired, Manning and his teammates swarmed the field in jubilation, while in the stands the fan who had blamed Accorsi now tried to kiss him.

Vindication

Only ten weeks after being described as "Eli the Terrible" by newspaper headlines, Manning stood at the pinnacle of the football world. He completed 19 of 34 passes for 255 yards and two touchdowns, gaining him the Most Valuable Player honor, the same award Peyton received only one year earlier. By tossing the winning pass in the game's last minute, he joined legendary Joe Montana as one of only two quarterbacks in Super Bowl history to accomplish the feat.

"The guys on this team and the run we've made, it's hard to believe—it really is," gushed Manning after the game. "The drive

For his 255 yards and 2 touchdowns Manning was named the Super Bowl's Most Valuable Player.

at the end, there were so many clutch plays by so many guys. It is an unbelievable game and an unbelievable feeling."[85]

He had reason to be elated. With the Super Bowl victory, Manning finally stood as a champion in his own right. He had shaken off errors and sloppy play, criticism from teammates, and caustic remarks from fans. He was Eli Manning, Super Bowl champion, not because he was anyone's son or brother but because of his talent and leadership.

"He's not Peyton Manning's little brother," said Strahan. "He's not Eli who slumps. None of that. Eli Manning is the world champion. I hope everybody remembers that, respects that, and understands that, because this team goes nowhere without him. Eli Manning has taken us to the Super Bowl and Eli Manning has won it for us."[86]

Praise from a teammate like Strahan was one thing; praise from an older brother is another. Peyton could not say enough about Eli's performance, especially how he handled the last-minute drive to earn the victory. "People always ask me who my favorite player is. I always say, 'It's my little brother,'" stated Peyton. "I promise you he was just as calm in that two-minute drill as he was in week four in the first quarter. That's the best characteristic he has and it's a great trait in quarterbacks."[87]

Eli Manning spent the night after winning the Super Bowl in deep reflection. While his teammates drank champagne and celebrated their victory, Manning returned to his hotel room at an early hour to watch replays of the game. He watched the whole game, but replayed the final two minutes time and time again, enjoying the images of how he brought the team from defeat to victory.

He finally knew what it felt like to be a champion.

Marriage and the Future

Conditions off the field matched the contentment Manning experienced on the gridiron. Since his Mississippi days he had dated Abby McGrew, a fashion designer. He proposed to her during the regular season in 2007, and three months after the

Manning married fashion designer Abby McGrew in 2008.

Super Bowl the two married in a sunset ceremony on a Cabo San Lucas, Mexico, beach. It was a quiet affair, with family and close friends attending.

Lending a Hand

Manning also joins his father and brothers each year at the Manning Passing Academy, a football camp in Thibodaux, Louisiana. The four instruct junior high and high school athletes in the proper way to throw a football and conduct an offense. The Mannings hope to help young players blossom into outstanding athletes as well as well-mannered individuals.

As much as possible for a public figure, Manning also keeps his charitable endeavors low-key. He and Peyton contributed time and money to their hometown of New Orleans after Hurricane Katrina ripped through Louisiana, loading water, Gatorade, diapers, and baby formula onto pallets. They talked to media outlets about the necessity for everyone to lend a hand and about how moved they were with the area's plight. "It's hard to watch what's happened to the city, people with no place to go, up to their waists in water," stated Eli. "We just wanted to do something extra, so we set up this plan to help some of these people."[88]

Besides his work after Hurricane Katrina, he also raises funds for the Eli Manning Children's Clinic at the Blair E. Batson Hospital for Children in Jackson, Mississippi. He had been moved by what he saw during a visit to the hospital and pledged his time and money. His father, Archie, agreed to help him gather donations for children. Also, Eli and his wife Abby donated money to create the Eli and Abby Manning Birthing Center at St. Vincent's Hospital in New York.

In addition to his charity efforts, Manning prepared for the coming football season. When training camp ended, analysts predicted another winning year for the Giants and posted them as early favorites to reach another Super Bowl.

Manning and the team started in championship fashion by sweeping their first four games. Coach Coughlin attributed much of their success to the confidence gained from the Super Bowl triumph. "Anytime you have that experience, and it's a positive one and you perform as he did," Coughlin explained of his quarterback, "it's obviously a very good boost of confidence. And I think it gives him and all of us the idea that going forward we can do nothing but get better."[89]

Manning seemed more relaxed as well. He started his annual Halloween party that he hosts for the team, an affair in which players dress in outlandish costumes and have fun. The joviality helped forge a tighter bond among the Giants players. "He had gone through some rough times," Strahan said of Manning, "but it's parties like these that go far in reinforcing our devotion to each other."[90]

The Giants swept seven of the next eight games to post a league-best 11–1 record before losing three of their final four games. Despite the sour ending, Manning had again helped his team to the playoffs with a 12–4 record, earning Offensive Player of the Month in November for his efforts. Their hopes of a second Super Bowl ended in the second round of the playoffs when the Giants dropped a 23–11 affair to the Philadelphia Eagles.

Manning may have missed a second championship, but he gained the respect of his football peers by registering some of his best numbers. He completed 60 percent of his passes, the highest of his career, and threw only ten interceptions. For the first time as a professional, Manning was named to the Pro Bowl team, designating him as one of the league's premier all-stars.

"You always want to be considered to be elite and play to the best of your abilities to be recognized across the league for what you are doing," Manning said. "It is such an honor having great players that are out there to be chosen by the fans and by the players and coaches."[91]

Peyton—an annual participant in the Pro Bowl—had invited Eli in the past to accompany him to the game, but Eli had always turned his brother down. He would join the festivities when he had earned it. "Peyton has invited me before," Manning says, "but I wanted to go when I made it on my own."[92]

Honors and acclaim had finally come to Eli Manning. He had successfully labored to be the best person and athlete he could be, and in quietly and efficiently going about his work he fashioned an all-star career of his own, in the process gaining the respect of fellow athletes, the recognition of fans, and the increased admiration of family.

"I never doubted that Eli would have this success and win championships," says Ernie Accorsi. "But I really believe the best is yet to come."[93]

Chapter 1: Football Runs in the Family

1. Archie and Peyton Manning, with John Underwood, *Manning*, New York: Harper Entertainment, 2000, p. 64.
2. Quoted in Ralph Vacchiano, *Eli Manning: The Making of a Quarterback*, New York: Skyhorse, 2008, pp. 22, 27.
3. Quoted in Vacchiano, *Eli Manning*, p. 22.
4. Manning, *Manning*, p. 173.
5. Quoted in Karen Crouse, "Eli Manning Took Cues from Mother," *New York Times*, January 29, 2008, www.nytimes.com/2008/01/29/sports/football/29manning.html.
6. Manning, *Manning*, p. 158.
7. Quoted in Manning, *Manning*, p. 299.
8. Quoted in Crouse, "Eli Manning Took Cues from Mother," p. 3.
9. Quoted in Vacchiano, *Eli Manning*, p. 30.
10. Quoted in Manning, *Manning*, p. 329.
11. Quoted in Manning, *Manning*, p. 303.
12. Quoted in Manning, *Manning*, p. 305.
13. Manning, *Manning*, p. 229.
14. Quoted in Clay Chandler, "Manning Nears Close of His Career," *Daily Mississippian*, November 20, 2003.
15. Quoted in Chandler, "Manning Nears Close of His Career."
16. Quoted in Joe Drape, "Eli Manning Inherits the Reins at Ole Miss," *New York Times*, October 19, 2001, www.nytimes.com/2001/10/19/sports/college-football-eli-manning-inherits-the-reins-at-ole-miss.html.
17. Quoted in Vacchiano, *Eli Manning*, p. 26.

Chapter 2: Steps Up His Game

18. Quoted in Peter Ross, "Ole Miss' Manning: A Golden Arm and a Sterling Pedigree," *Daily Mississippian*, August 31, 2001, www.highbeam.com/doc/1P1-46600277.html.
19. Quoted in Drape, "Eli Manning Inherits the Reins at Ole Miss."
20. Quoted in Ross, "Ole Miss' Manning."
21. Quoted in Ross, "Ole Miss' Manning."

22. Quoted in Ross, "Ole Miss' Manning."
23. Quoted in Ross, "Ole Miss' Manning."
24. Manning, *Manning*, p. 21.
25. Quoted in Ross, "Ole Miss' Manning."
26. Quoted in Peter Ross, "Rebs Roll," *Daily Mississippian*, October 15, 2001.
27. Drape, "Eli Manning Inherits the Reins at Ole Miss."
28. Drape, "Eli Manning Inherits the Reins at Ole Miss."
29. Quoted in Ross, "Ole Miss' Manning."

Chapter 3: Great Expectations

30. Quoted in Kyle Veazey, "No Bones About It—Florida Is a Marked Foe," *Daily Mississippian*, October 3, 2002.
31. Quoted in Vacchiano, *Eli Manning*, p. 14.
32. Quoted in Kyle Veazey, "Eli's Big Decision Will Wait Until After Bowl," *Daily Mississippian*, December 3, 2002.
33. Quoted in Ray Glier, "Manning Keeps Heisman Hype on Field," *New York Times*, July 31, 2003, www.nytimes.com/2003/07/31/sports/college-football-manning-keeps-heisman-hype-on-field.html.
34. Quoted in Kyle Veazey, "Eli Offers a Simple Explanation: 'I Wanted to Stay,'" *Daily Mississippian*, January 17, 2003.
35. Quoted in Glier, "Manning Keeps Heisman Hype on Field."
36. Quoted in Manning, *Manning*, p. 303.
37. Quoted in Steven Godfrey, "For One More Year, Eli Manning Lives Under the Microscope," *Daily Mississippian*, September 12, 2003.
38. Quoted in Steven Godfrey, "Rebel Run Culminates with Cotton Bowl Victory," *Daily Mississippian*, January 7, 2004.
39. Quoted in Lynn Zinser, "Manning's Day Gets Miles Better After a Trade to the Giants," *New York Times*, April 25, 2004, www.nytimes.com/2004/04/25/sports/pro-football-manning-s-day-gets-miles-better-after-a-trade-to-the-giants.html.
40. Quoted in Zinser, "Manning's Day Gets Miles Better."

Chapter 4: Playing in the NFL

41. Quoted in Lynn Zinser, "Manning's Fast Signing Is a Bonus All Around," *New York Times*, July 30, 2004, www.nytimes.com/

2004/07/30/sports/pro-football-manning-s-fast-signing-is-a-bonus-all-around.html.

42. Michael Strahan, with Jay Glazer, *Inside the Helmet: Life as a Sunday Afternoon Warrior*, New York: Gotham, 2007, pp. 136–37.

43. Quoted in Vacchiano, *Eli Manning*, p. 76.

44. Quoted in Vacchiano, *Eli Manning*, p. 32.

45. Strahan, *Inside the Helmet*, p. 138.

46. Quoted in Lynn Zinser, "Present Imperfect, Future Is Manning," *New York Times*, November 22, 2004, www.nytimes.com/2004/11/22/sports/football/22giants.html.

47. Quoted in Zinser, "Present Imperfect, Future Is Manning."

48. Quoted in Zinser, "Present Imperfect, Future Is Manning."

49. Quoted in Zinser, "Present Imperfect, Future Is Manning."

50. Quoted in Vacchiano, *Eli Manning*, p. 106.

51. Quoted in Vacchiano, *Eli Manning*, pp. 106–107.

52. Quoted in Jeff Zillgitt, "Giants' Manning Licks His Wounds," *USA Today*, December 12, 2004, www.usatoday.com/sports/columnist/zillgitt/2004-12-12-zillgitt_x.htm.

53. Quoted in Vacchiano, *Eli Manning*, p. 33.

54. Quoted in Dave Caldwell, "Manning Helps in Developing Giant Game Plan," *New York Times*, December 17, 2004, www.nytimes.com/2004/12/17/sports/football/17giants.html.

55. Quoted in Lynn Zinser, "Reason to Cheer Amid a Chorus of Doubts," *New York Times*, December 19, 2004, www.nytimes.com/2004/12/19/sports/football/19giants.html.

56. Quoted in Jerry Magee, "Looking Out for No. 1," *San Diego Union-Tribune*, September 21, 2005, www.signonsandiego.com/sports/chargers/20050921-9999-1s21manning1.html.

57. Quoted in Vacchiano, *Eli Manning*, p. 35.

58. Quoted in Vacchiano, *Eli Manning*, p. 32.

59. Judy Battista, "Manning's Learning Curve Loses Its Arc," *New York Times*, October 3, 2005, www.nytimes.com/2005/10/03/sports/football/03giants.html.

60. Quoted in Battista, "Manning's Learning Curve Loses Its Arc."

61. Quoted in John Branch, "Manning's Career Could Use an Off-Season Exorcism," *New York Times*, January 11, 2006, www.nytimes.com/2006/01/11/sports/football/11giants.html.

Chapter 5: Time to Prove Himself

62. Quoted in Warren St. John, "The Brother Bowl," *New York Times*, August 20, 2006, www.nytimes.com/2006/08/20/sports/playmagazine/20manning.html.

63. Quoted in John Branch, "Third and Ready?" *New York Times*, September 3, 2006, www.nytimes.com/2006/09/03/sports/football/03giants.html.

64. Quoted in Vacchiano, *Eli Manning*, p. 122.

65. Quoted in Vacchiano, *Eli Manning*, p. 118.

66. Strahan, *Inside the Helmet*, p. 4.

67. Quoted in Associated Press, "Where's the Brotherly Love?" ESPN.com, September 10, 2006, http://sports.espn.go.com/nfl/recap?gameId=260910019.

68. Quoted in John Branch, "Manning Doesn't Lose His Cool During the Giants' Comeback," *New York Times*, September 19, 2006, http://query.nytimes.com/gst/fullpage.html?res=9D07E1DA1031F93AA2575AC0A9609C8B63.

69. Quoted in Vacchiano, *Eli Manning*, p. 168.

70. Quoted in John Branch, "Franchise in Flux, a Quarterback at a Standstill," *New York Times*, January 7, 2007, www.nytimes.com/2007/01/07/sports/football/07giants.html.

71. Quoted in Branch, "Franchise in Flux."

72. Quoted in Vacchiano, *Eli Manning*, pp. 209–10.

73. Quoted in Vacchiano, *Eli Manning*, pp. 166–67.

74. Quoted in Michael Eisen, "Archie Shares Thoughts on Manning Bowl," Giants.com, May 12, 2006, www.giants.com/news/headlines/story.asp?story_id=15577.

75. Quoted in Vacchiano, *Eli Manning*, p. 177.

76. Quoted in Vacchiano, *Eli Manning*, p. 223.

Chapter 6: "The Best Is Yet to Come"

77. Quoted in Associated Press, "Manning, Giants Head to Super Bowl for Rematch with Pats," ESPN.com, January 20, 2008, http://scores.espn.go.com/nfl/recap?gameId=280120009.

78. Associated Press, "Manning, Giants Head to Super Bowl for Rematch with Pats."

79. Quoted in Vacchiano, *Eli Manning*, p. 238.

80. Quoted in Vacchiano, *Eli Manning*, p. 249.

81. Quoted in Ralph Vacchiano, "Giants Stun Patriots to Win Super Bowl," *New York Daily News*, February 5, 2008, www. nydailynews.com/sports/football/giants/2008/02/03/2008-02-03_giants_stun_patriots_to_win_super_bowl-2.html.

82. Quoted in Ralph Vacchiano, "Eli Manning Turns Career Around to Become News' Sportsperson of 2008," *New York Daily News*, January 3, 2009, www.nydailynews.com/sports/football/giants/2009/01/03/2009-01-03_eli_manning_turns_career_around_to_becom.html.

83. Quoted in Vacchiano, *Eli Manning*, p. 254.

84. Quoted in Vacchiano, "Giants Stun Patriots to Win Super Bowl."

85. Quoted in Greg Garber, "Eli, Monster Defense Power Giants to Shocking Super Bowl Victory," ESPN.com, February 3, 2008, http://sports.espn.go.com/nfl/recap?gameId=280203017.

86. Quoted in Vacchiano, *Eli Manning*, p. 266.

87. Quoted in Vacchiano, *Eli Manning*, pp. 37, 266.

88. Quoted in Marsha Walton, "Manning Brothers Team Up for Katrina Relief," CNN.com, September 5, 2005, www.cnn.com/2005/US/09/04/mannings.relief/index.html.

89. Quoted in Ralph Vacchiano, "Experts Say Giants QB Eli Manning Surpasses Brother Peyton," *New York Daily News*, October 8, 2008, www.nydailynews.com/sports/football/giants/2008/10/07/2008-10-07_experts_say_giants_qb_eli_manning_surpas.html.

90. Quoted in Strahan, *Inside the Helmet*, p. 80.

91. Quoted in Michael Eisen, "Six Giants Named to Pro Bowl," Giants.com, December 16, 2008, www.giants.com/news/headlines/story.asp?story_id=33269&print=yes.

92. Quoted in Eisen, "Six Giants Named to Pro Bowl."

93. Quoted in Vacchiano, "Eli Manning Turns Career Around to Become News' Sportsperson of 2008."

1981

Eli Nelson Manning is born in New Orleans, Louisiana.

1999

Decides to attend the University of Mississippi (Ole Miss).

2001

Starts in his first college football game against Murray State University.

2002

Quarterbacks Ole Miss to victory in the Independence Bowl.

2003

Finishes third in the voting for the Heisman Trophy.

2004

On January 2, leads Mississippi to a major victory in the Cotton Bowl; on November 21, starts his first game as quarterback for the New York Giants.

2005

Plays in his first NFL playoff contest.

2006

Loses 23–21 to brother Peyton and the Colts in the "Manning Bowl".

2007

Earns his first postseason win; earns a spot in the Super Bowl with a win over the Green Bay Packers.

2008

Receives the Most Valuable Player award for leading the Giants to a win in Super Bowl XLII; on April 19, marries Abby McGrew in Mexico.

For More Information

Books

Matt Christopher, *On the Field with Peyton and Eli Manning*. New York: Little, Brown, 2008. This is a dual biography for an upper-elementary audience.

Matt Doeden, *Eli Manning*. Minneapolis, MN: Twenty-First Century, 2008. Doeden delivers a superb summary of Manning's life for middle-elementary students. He sprinkles brief quotes throughout the narrative.

Hugh Hudson, *Back-to-Back: Super Bowl Champions Peyton and Eli Manning*. New York: Price Stern Sloan, 2008. Written for the middle-elementary students, this book depicts the Manning brothers' successful careers, culminated with Super Bowl victories.

Archie and Peyton Manning, with John Underwood, *Manning*. New York: HarperEntertainment, 2000. This valuable book contains significant information on the Manning family. It especially reveals how the parents, Archie and Olivia, raised their three sons to be decent, hard-working individuals. The book offers numerous anecdotes about the parents and their relationships with Cooper, Peyton, and Eli.

New York Post, Eli Manning and Big Blue. New York: Triumph, 2008. This book appeared shortly after Manning's Super Bowl victory. Compiled by one of New York's newspapers, it consists of different sections pertaining to Manning or the Giants. Numerous photographs accompany the text.

Ralph Vacchiano, *Eli Manning: The Making of a Quarterback*. New York: Skyhorse, 2008. Award-winning New York sportswriter Ralph Vacchiano covered the Giants for the *New York Daily News*. In this book he delivers valuable insights and information on Eli Manning and the inside workings of the Giants football team.

Internet Sources

Associated Press, "Eli Manning Looking for First Postseason Win," SportingNews, January 1, 2008, www.sportingnews.com/nfl/articles/20080101/982629-p.html.

Kristin Boehm, "Eli Manning and Abby McGrew Wed on the Beach," *People*, April 20, 2008, www.people.com/people/article/0,,20193253,00.html.

John Branch, "Manning Doesn't Lose His Cool During the Giants' Comeback," *New York Times*, September 19, 2006, www.nytimes.com/2006/09/19/sports/football/19giants.html.

Dave Caldwell, "Manning Helps in Developing Giant Game Plan," *New York Times*, December 17, 2004, www.nytimes.com/2004/12/17/sports/football/17giants.html.

Joe Drape, "Eli Manning Inherits the Reins at Ole Miss," *New York Times*, October 19, 2001, www.nytimes.com/2001/10/19/sports/college-football-eli-manning-inherits-the-reins-at-ole-miss.html.

Michael Eisen, "Archie Shares Thoughts on Manning Bowl," Giants.com, May 12, 2006, www.giants.com/news/headlines/story.asp?story_id=15577.

Friends of Children's Hospital, "An Evening with the Mannings 2008," Friends of Children's Hospital, http://foch.org/mannings.php.

Greg Garber, "Eli, Monster Defense Power Giants to Shocking Super Bowl Victory," ESPN.com, February 3, 2008, http://sports.espn.go.com/nfl/recap?gameId=280203017.

Adam Sternbergh, "Underdog," *New York Magazine*, January 27, 2008, http://nymag.com/news/features/43338.

Warren St. John, "The Brother Bowl," *New York Times*, August 20, 2006, www.nytimes.com/2006/08/20/sports/playmagazine/20manning.html.

Ralph Vacchiano, "Eli Manning Turns Career Around to Become News' Sportsperson of 2008," *New York Daily News*, January 3, 2009, www.nydailynews.com/sports/football/giants/2009/01/03/2009-01-03_eli_manning_turns_career_around_to_becom.html.

Marsha Walton, "Manning Brothers Team Up for Katrina Relief," CNN.com, September 5, 2005, www.cnn.com/2005/US/09/04/mannings.relief/index.html.

Lynn Zinser, "Manning's Day Gets Miles Better After a Trade to the Giants," *New York Times*, April 25, 2004, www.nytimes.com/2004/04/25/sports/pro-football-manning-s-day-gets-miles-better-after-a-trade-to-the-giants.html.

Web Sites

Manning Passing Academy (www.manningpassingacademy.com). This is the Web site for the Manning Passing Academy, a football camp sponsored by Archie Manning and his three sons. The site offers information about the camp and its areas of instruction.

National Football League (www.nfl.com). This is the Web site of the National Football League. It provides all the basic statistics and facts about every player in NFL history, including Eli, Peyton, and Archie Manning.

New York Giants (www.giants.com). The official Web site for the New York Giants offers information on Manning and other Giants athletes, the history of the team, podcasts, and much more, including game statistics for every contest involving Eli Manning.

John F. Wukovits is a retired junior high school teacher and writer from Trenton, Michigan, who specializes in history and biography. Besides biographies of Anne Frank, Jim Carrey, Michael J. Fox, Stephen King, and Martin Luther King Jr. for Lucent Books, he has written biographies about Clifton Sprague, Barry Sanders, Tim Allen, Jack Nicklaus, Vince Lombardi, and Wyatt Earp. He is also the author of many books about World War II, including *Pacific Alamo: The Battle for Wake Island* (2003), *One Square Mile of Hell: The Battle for Tarawa* (2006), *Eisenhower: A Biography* (2006), and *American Commando* (2009). A graduate of the University of Notre Dame, Wukovits is the father of three daughters—Amy, Julie, and Karen—and the grandfather of Matthew, Megan, Emma, and Kaitlyn.

Property of
Newkirk High School